THE ADVENTURES OF NOAH MELVILLE

The Wizard of Time

JOHN VERISSIMO

authorHOUSE®

AuthorHouse™
1663 Liberty Drive
Bloomington, IN 47403
www.authorhouse.com
Phone: 1-800-839-8640

First published by AuthorHouse 11/16/2011

ISBN: 978-1-4678-7034-4 (e)
ISBN: 978-1-4678-7035-1 (hc)
ISBN: 978-1-4678-7036-8 (sc)

Library of Congress Control Number: 2011960722

Printed in the United States of America

Table of Contents

Eight Weeks Earlier … 5

Carly's Secret 19

The Big Launch 29

Calm Before the Storm 39

No More Secrets 49

Rebuilding the *Drifter* 55

The Big Plan of Attack 63

The Hunt Begins 69

The Escape 79

The Big Jump in Time 89

Captain Bell and the *Huntress* 93

Noah Takes Command of the *Huntress* 103

The Hunt for Captain Bell 109

The Wizard Keeps His Promise 123

The Voyage Home 133

Mayor Smith Keeps His Word 141

Heading Back into the Past 149

The crew woke not to the smell of breakfast cooking, but to the sound of thundering cannons in the near distance. Noah sprang out of bed along with the rest of the crew. Simon was still sleeping—he could sleep through anything. Hunter and Carly made their way up onto the bow. Cappy ran up the stairs leading to Noah. There, Noah stood by the helm looking through the spyglass, trying to catch his breath. He was watching two ships battling in the distance. The smoke filling the air made it very hard to see, but Noah saw the British flag flying at the top of the mast on one of them. The British ship was fighting with another larger ship, a pirate ship from the looks of it. The whole crew was up on deck now and eager to help.

Noah yelled, "Haul the anchors- quickly!"

Cappy ran down by the mast with the crew.

Noah yelled, "Raise the sails! Faster! Let's go!"

Up the sails went just as the anchors broke out of the water. They were on their way to help the queen's ship. The *Huntress* was ready for battle, and since it was the queen's ship, they had better help. They were getting closer but still moved too slowly.

Noah looked at Carly. "Now would be a good time," he said.

Dizzy looked at her. "For what?"

Carly smiled. Her eyes began to glow bright green as she lifted her arms into the air. She pushed forward with her hands as she filled the sails with wind. The ship immediately picked up its pace. She was really moving now.

Hunter yelled up to Noah, "What side are we firing the cannons from?"

Noah looked down. "Both! Both sides!"

The crew looked at him with disbelief—all but Cappy, that is.

Smiling, Cappy said, "We are going right between them! Isn't that right, son?"

They all looked up as if Noah were crazy. Noah was too focused on what he was doing to answer the question. He called to Hunter, "When I tell you, drop the anchors on both sides of the ship to slow it down, and then the sails, you hear?"

They managed to squeeze themselves midway between the two ships.

In the midst of smoke and cannonballs flying in every direction, Noah yelled, "Now!"

In a flash, the anchors dropped, and down came the sails. Simon, now fully awake, pulled the British flag up as fast as he could, so they would not fire on the *Huntress*. As the ship came to a slow stop, Carly and Dizzy turned to face the pirate ship. Both fell to their knees. Noah and his crew dropped to the deck and took cover for what was to come. Their arms went up. Both their eyes began to glow that brilliant yellow green. Now, with one push forward with their hands, a surge of energy flew through the air, striking the pirate ship as if being made to do something against its will. The ship let out a ghostly screech as it slowly began to list on its side. The pirates held on as they saw sails being ripped away in a frenzy of destruction. Carly and Dizzy unleashed their powers even harder. The pirates were no match for them. Cappy yelled for them to stop, but there was no holding them back now. Both became stronger and stronger. The bright glow coming from them made it hard to see. Noah and Cappy yelled with all their might, pleading with them to stop. The ship was on the verge of rolling. As she leaned farther over, Noah and his crew could see the grass that had grown on the bottom of this once-fierce vessel. Was there no coming back? Soon, water was rolling off the keel.

Eight Weeks Earlier ...
In the small town of Silver Shell

The bell rang, and Noah ran out the door and straight to his locker to get his fishing pole and the rest of the things he needed. Noah's father worked at the local boatyard. He was a painter there. Noah loved to go straight down to the old boatyard to see his father and what new sailboats were there. Noah always made time to run to the end of the pier to see the *Raven* anchored out in the harbor.

The *Raven* was an old sailing ship that at one time chased the pirates out of the harbor, keeping the town safe. The ship was over a hundred years old.

Noah could only see adventure in this old ship. Just the thought of chasing pirates across the ocean made him smile.

But as history had it, the *Raven* had a run-in with a ship called *Dark Spirit*. This pirate ship had a powerful wizard. *Raven* and its brave crew battled the most powerful pirate ship that sailed the ocean. The battle was not long. *Raven* was nearly ready to lose. Just then, its captain sent down the first dory with some of his crew to escape. Before the *Raven* could send down another lifeboat, *Dark Spirit* stopped its attack. The captain of the *Raven* could not understand why. The *Dark Spirit* had won the battle. Just then, the *Dark Spirit* turned, and with a bright flash of light, it was gone. When the *Dark Spirit* jumped through time, the small lifeboat went with it. Soon after, the *Raven* would start the sail home, wondering what happened to the crew that disappeared in the lifeboat. That was the last time *Raven* had sailed.

Knapsack in one hand and his grandfather's fishing pole in the other, Noah headed to see his father.

Noah's mom worked at the local laundry in town. They were a very poor family, considering they lived by the water. Most of Noah's schoolmates came from rich families.

Noah was a rather tall young man with dark eyes and long hair that he wore in a ponytail. Noah loved his worn-out jeans and black leather vest. Noah didn't go anywhere without that vest. His boots looked like he'd walked a million miles in them, but the young man would not trade them for the world. Noah was a lonely child and spent most of his time alone, dreaming of having a sailboat of his own.

There was a marina for all the sailboats next to the boatyard. Most of the kids from school had sailboats, and every day after school, they all went down to the marina and took the small sailboats out in the harbor for a sail. They were allowed to go outside the harbor but not beyond the Forbidden Islands. There was a ghost ship that had been seen there, mostly by the old-timers of the town. The story of the ghost ship had been told for many years by the sailors.

There was a seal that came every year to the harbor to visit. Noah hoped he would be back soon. The seal normally came to the pier and watched Noah fish every year, but Noah had not seen him this year and wondered if he would return. After all, Noah had no friends. He just didn't seem to fit in with the others. But Charlie, the seal, didn't seem to mind. Noah named the seal after his grandpa, whom he missed very much.

Noah would spend day after day watching the other children sail their boats throughout the harbor as he fished off the pier, hoping to catch a big fish to show his father. Noah really wanted his own sailboat, but his family was poor, and they could not give him one.

Just then, his pole curled right over and began to crack.

Noah had finally caught the fish his father would be proud of. He kept reeling and reeling the fish in, but the old pole just would not pull the fish to him. All he could think about was how proud his father would be. Finally, after what seemed to be a year to the young boy, he could see his prize near. Just as the fish popped his head out of the water with Noah barely hanging on to get his fish, the pole broke in half. Noah was quick and grabbed the line to try to keep his prize. He had not given up. His father would be so proud. The line on the pole was older than Noah's father and wasn't going to stay together much longer. Then, it happened. The line broke, and Noah went flying backward. All the children from school, who were watching the whole thing from their fancy sailboats, began laughing. With his head down, Noah picked up his bag and headed home. He walked slowly, thinking about how he would break the news that he'd lost his grandpa's fishing pole. The walk seemed to take forever.

Noah lived around people with sailboats; there was one in every yard. As he walked home, some of the children from the marina were getting dropped off at their homes, all smiling with laughter at watching Noah with that fish earlier.

After some time, and feeling sadder than he had ever felt before, he took a different way home so he would not be seen by all the children from the marina. He found himself walking down a dirt road he had never walked down. He looked in the yards now that he could raise his head without people seeing his face. There were some men working on their sailboats, getting them ready to go in the water to sail the ocean.

Noah wanted so badly to have his own, but he knew it was impossible.

The sky turned dark. Rain was coming.

There was a big, angry dog in the yard to the side of Noah. That dog looked at Noah like he was a steak. He wanted a piece of Noah for sure. The dog barked wildly, pulling hard on his long leash.

Rain was coming down in buckets. Noah wasn't having a good day.

Then, the large dog broke his leash, and after Noah he went. Noah began running—almost right out of his shoes. Splashing through the puddles, he ran faster and faster. There was a turn coming, but that dog was catching up. Noah turned the corner around a tall fence, and right behind him, so did the dog. Noah looked back as the dog's long leash caught the fence. Finally, the chase was over.

Breathing hard, he slowed to a walk once again. After all that, he walked down another wrong road. It was a dead end. One good thing was that the rain had stopped. Now chilled to the bone, he looked around, dreading having to walk back the other way when he saw an old, run-down house with a large shed and what looked like boat parts here and there. It was really hard to tell, because the grass was as tall as he was. As he turned to begin his long walk back up the bumpy dirt road, he caught something out of the corner of his eye. He stopped and stood there a moment. He began to turn very slowly to see if what he'd thought he had seen was real. He stopped, afraid to be disappointed once again, and he turned back toward the road and began to walk. Before he could put his foot down after one step, he stopped again. He said, "Okay, I will close my eyes and turn to open them." So Noah closed his eyes and turned slowly. His head came to a stop, and then he stood there with his eyes closed, afraid to even look. He opened one eye very slowly, and there it was, though he could barely see it from all the overgrown grass and trees. There was an old sailboat just sitting on the side of the old barn. It looked as if it had been there forever, but in Noah's eyes, this was the most beautiful thing he had ever seen. Noah had to have it. Why would anyone want it?

The next day, Noah took the same way home after school so that he could take yet another look at the old sailboat.

After a long walk in the wrong direction, he came to the house where the boat lay hidden in the forest of grass. He paced back and forth in front of the house, turning and looking every now and again. What would he say to the person?

A truck pulled up, and a man jumped out. It was the food market truck from town. The man opened the back doors, pulled some bags of food out, and headed for the forest of grass. He pushed his way through the tall grass and up to the porch of the old home. After the man knocked on the door three or four times, someone finally opened it.

There stood an old man. His beard was long and gray, just like the hair on his head. He was an old gent who stood over six feet tall, and he was bulky, as well. He turned and glanced at Noah with his dark brown eyes. He looked angry for some reason.

The delivery man took his money for the food and wished the old man a good day. Noah heard him call the old gent "Cappy." *What kind of name was that?* thought Noah.

Well, it was now or never, so Noah headed for the house and pushed aside all the grass, soon to be at the door.

Noah had never been so nervous as he was now, standing in front of the door. He gave a knock. There was nothing. Noah knew the man was there, so he knocked again and again. The man just wouldn't answer. Noah started walking back to the road when the man opened the door. Noah turned to look. The man was looking at Noah as if he had done something wrong. Finally, Noah asked the man if he would sell the old boat on the side of the barn.

He looked at the man, waiting. There was silence between the two.

"She will never sail again," Cappy finally said, referring to the boat. He then told Noah to get off his property as he slammed the door.

Noah was heartbroken. He had many plans for this boat. Noah walked toward the street, his head down. Yet another dream would not come true.

Noah went to school the next day, and as soon as the bell rang—like any other day—he headed for the boatyard. But on his way out the door, one of the kids from the marina said hello. Noah was shy, since it was Carly.

Carly was a tomboy all the way. She was rather short, all of five feet tall. She had wavy, bright-red hair down to her shoulders, and she had a few freckles on her pale face. But there was something about her eyes. They were deep green and almost glowed. Carly wore a vest, as well—black like Noah's. Seemed all the kids did. She had her own boat down at the marina next to all the other sailboats.

Carly was a bit of a loner, as well. She did have friends, but not close ones. You see, the adults told an old story about her great-grandfather from time to time. The great-grandfather was said to be a wizard—like his father before. The town had feared this man. Some said his eyes had a strange red glow, and he stood nearly seven feet tall. He looked down upon you with his glowing red eyes, they said. One could see his white, snarly hair from under his dark, tall hat and creepy, dark robe. As legend had it, he looked into your soul. It was said that he vanished one day but promised to return when it was time—time for what, nobody knew. Noah knew of this legend, but none of this made any sense to him. Carly had been adopted, so how could they know who her great-grandfather was, unless they knew something she didn't?

Carly asked if he was going fishing down at the pier.

Noah had no fishing pole anymore. That big fish put an end to his fishing days.

"Not fishing," he said, "but I'm going down to have a look at the boats."

Carly asked if she could come, since she was going down there anyway.

They walked and talked about sailing all the way down there, and Carly invited Noah to come for a ride on her boat. Noah was speechless—he didn't want her to know he didn't know how to sail. Carly seemed to know this anyway.

Before Noah could say a word, Carly said, "Great, let's get moving so we can catch the wind."

Off went Noah on his first sailboat ride ever. He was in his glory, and Carly showed him the ropes of how to sail. It didn't take long, and she had him doing everything on his own.

Carly said, "I can't believe how well you sail, and you have never been on a boat before."

She knew he was special. Most people took years to learn

and do what Noah did in a day. He was a natural—born to the sea.

While they were sailing, they talked of many things. Noah told Carly of the big, old sailboat he had found. He also told her how mean the old man was. Carly told him not to take "No" for an answer and to never give up on anything in life. Noah bowed his head. They brought the boat back and tied it to the pier.

As they stood on the pier saying their farewells, Noah said, "Thank you for such a day."

Charlie popped his head up out of the water and splashed Noah. Carly couldn't believe the seal was Noah's friend, but they had to go home before dark. They both waved Charlie a good-bye. Carly told Noah she would see him in school and walked the other way.

On the way home, Noah was all smiles. What a day! All the trash cans were out for the morning to be picked up. Just as Noah was about to turn the corner, he saw a box on the side of one of the garbage cans with a tall stack of books in it. He stopped because he saw that one of them had a sailboat on the cover. He grabbed the stack of books and continued walking. The day couldn't get any better. Now with some books to read up on sailing, Noah couldn't wait to get home and take a peek. He has looking though the stack while walking when he found an old book, so full of dust he barely could see the cover. Noah took a big breath and blew the dust off the old book. Just then, Noah stopped. He stared at the cover. This went on for at least five minutes when he said out loud, "I can't believe it."

On the cover of the book was the old man's house—Cappy's house. But there was no tall grass, and it was beautiful. When Noah looked inside, he saw a picture of the barn. Cappy was a boat builder. Noah could not believe this. There was the boat on the side of the barn, but it looked as if it could just fly with the beauty it held. Noah began to read the story, finding out that Cappy's wife had died and the boatbuilding had stopped. The story explained that Cappy built the fastest and most seaworthy boats ever to be built, and they were going to miss him in the boating world. Noah now knew why Cappy seemed so mean—he had given up on life. Some people just gave up when they thought there was nothing left to live for.

Noah could not wait to show Carly, his new friend. As soon as the bell rang, he ran to find her. After looking all over, he spotted her down on her boat, guessing that he missed her at school.

With a big smile, Carly said hello. "I looked for you but didn't see you after school, Noah."

Smiling, Noah pulled out the book from his bag. Carly could not believe how well Cappy built boats.

She said, "I told you not to give up." She then read that Cappy had lost his wife. "Well, there you go, Noah. The man gave up. We will have to show him there's still something to live for." Off they went, once again beginning the long walk.

They both rounded the corner to Cappy's house, and Noah pointed and said, "That's the one." So they began to walk to the door and Carly would show Noah how to get this man's attention. They knocked and knocked, but there was no answer. Noah's head went down again. He looked one more time at the book and slid it under the door. As Noah and Carly walked away, the door opened, and the man came out. Noah didn't know what to say, and Cappy could see this. He asked Noah if he had the skill to fix this boat that he wanted so badly. Noah didn't know what to say again. The man turned and began to go back in.

Noah said, "No, but I can sail, and I know you were the best builder in the world."

Cappy looked at him and said, "Now, why would I fix it?"

Noah paused a moment and then said, "I will do anything you ask of me."

Cappy wasn't prepared to deal with people, never mind some young kid.

While Noah and Cappy were talking, Carly sneaked around the barn to get a closer look at the boat that Noah wanted so badly. As she came closer to the boat, the grass seemed taller and taller, until it was well above her head. Just as she was about to turn back, she pushed a bunch of the forest-like grass to each side with two hands. She slowly looked up with her eyes as wide as could be.

This was no small boat—it was a schooner. Smaller she was, but much bigger than any of the sailboats from the marina. From the road, it looked small with the grass covering it. But this was a sailing machine, a real live a board that could sail around the world. What on earth was it doing just sitting here, hiding for decades? Carly walked around the boat, taking a really good look. She just couldn't believe that this incredible boat was to lie here, never to be used again. She made it to the other side of the boat. There on the ground was the large mast and boom, neatly stored away. Leaning against the barn were all the stay wires that held the mast and boom in place. She wondered if there were sails hidden somewhere for this boat. Carly knew Noah had found something incredible, and she had to help him get this boat. Carly wanted to help put it back together and sail it with Noah.

She ran back to the house to tell Noah what she had seen. She could see that Cappy and Noah were talking, but it didn't look good from the look on Cappy's face. She walked up to the porch. She was winded, and her face was as red as could be. She was covered in grass and dirt, and her hair looked like a weed farm. Noah turned to look at her, and as he turned back to Cappy, he had to swing his head around to take another look at her.

"What happened to you?" Noah asked.

Cappy said, "I know what happened. She went snooping in the backyard at the boat." Then Cappy asked Noah where he had gotten the book.

Noah told him it was in a pile of books on the side of the road. The old man looked down at the book once again. A tear ran down his face.

Cappy said, "You know, kids, this was a very long time ago." He thought of his wife that had always wanted children. He took a deep breath and said, "We will talk tomorrow, *but no promises!* Okay?"

The old man turned and walked into the house. Noah and Carly were thrilled with what Cappy had said. It wasn't a no, at least.

Noah and Carly went right from school to the old man's house the following day. They walked as fast as they could. Carly told Noah that the boat was much bigger than he'd thought. Noah didn't seem to give it any thought, but Carly knew they had their work cut out for them. After walking down all the bumpy dirt roads once again, they finally came to the old man's house. Carly was eager to run right up the stairs, but Noah had to pace a bit before he could confront Cappy.

"Let's go," Carly said. "He didn't say no, so let's go talk to the man."

Finally, Noah headed for the house, hoping not to be disappointed. They came to the door, and Noah stood there yet again. Carly rolled her eyes and decided to knock herself. It took a few times, but Cappy opened the door. There was the old man standing there once again, but he didn't seem so distant from them this time.

Cappy said, "I read the book and spent most of the night thinking about the story written within it."

Now, he didn't have any children, but his wife always wanted to have them, Cappy thought to himself once again. This ongoing thought seemed to weigh heavily on his mind. Cappy told Noah he would help. I guess he thought since his wife really wanted children, this would be a way to give her what she wanted in some way—by helping this young man and his sidekick. Noah smiled and didn't know what to say. Carly smiled, as well, and she knew more about this boat, seeing that she had sneaked around to take a look. Cappy told Noah that they had a lot of work to do on the old boat. The forest of grass would have to go, and the workshop in the barn would have to be cleaned up to take this project on.

Cappy told the kids, "Come back tomorrow, and we will start the project. Get a lot of rest. You know the saying—'be careful what you wish for.'"

Carly's Secret

Well, it was the weekend, and Noah went over to Carly's house to get her to start the new project—and a project it would be. But when Noah arrived, he saw Simon from the marina heading that way as well.

Now, Simon was the brain in school. He loved the ocean and studying the world charts of all of the places that he would sail someday. Simon's family had a little money—they were not rich, but they were a step up from poor. He was a tall, clumsy kid. Simon's glasses had thick lenses and a band to hold them on. But what got Noah was the tape holding them together. Noah was sure Simon's family could get him some new glasses. Simon had really short hair, close to being bald. For some reason, this young man always had a striped shirt and pants that were just too short. Now, Noah didn't care what people wore—or looked like, for that matter—and a friend was a friend to Noah.

Simon said hello as they walked toward Carly's house. Noah went for the door, and Simon called over to stop him.

Carly's mother didn't like her being around the boys, even though they were all fourteen.

Noah walked over to Simon and asked, "What's wrong?"

"Believe me, you don't want to meet the mother," said Simon.

So they went around the side of the house and looked for some pebbles to toss at Carly's bedroom window. They could hear her mother yelling up to Carly's room, "You're not leaving until your room is clean, young lady!"

So the boys were really quiet heading over to her window. They looked up, and before Simon could toss a rock, both of their jaws just dropped.

Everything was floating around in Carly's room. Well, Simon and Noah just looked at one another. The boys climbed up the lattice on the side of the house leading to Carly's window. There was Carly lying on the bed and reading a book. But everything was flying around the room. Drawers opened as the clothes floated in. Simon and Noah just looked at each other as their jaws dropped once again. There she was just reading a book as the room cleaned itself. Then all of a sudden, Carly felt someone looking at her. She turned, and her jaw dropped along with everything that was floating around the room.

Well, there was something to this story about her great-grandfather being some kind of wizard. It seemed that she had some powers of her own.

Carly popped up from the bed, and at the same time, both boys fell off the side of the house—it wasn't too far, but it was far enough. There was a thump to the ground followed by another thump.

Carly ran to the window to see if they were all right. The window opened, and Carly looked down at the boys.

"What happened?" she asked.

They just looked at her with a weird look on their faces. Carly knew there was no hiding the fact that she inherited her great-grandfather's powers. But what great-grandfather? She was adopted.

As Carly ran down her stairs and out the door to the boys, they were just getting up brushing off the dirt and grass.

Carly asked, "What's wrong?"

"Well, Carly," Noah said, "I thought I was seeing things but since Simon here seen the same. Well, were wondering just how all them things were floating around the room. I mean ... the room ... was cleaning itself."

Simon was still speechless to say the least.

Carly looked down, speechless for a moment herself. "Noah, you and Simon can never tell anyone what you just seen. The stories must be true! A few years ago, things began to happen."

"Like what?" asked Noah.

"Well, every time I really thought about something—like having to move something—it would begin to move on its own. Before I knew it, I could do a lot of things, but I have never told anyone about this," said Carly. She made the boys promise they would never repeat to anyone what she had told them.

Noah just looked at Carly and said, "I thought you were adopted."

"I was," said Carly. "I really don't know what to believe anymore. Someday, I hope to solve this puzzle of mine."

After that was over, Simon asked Carly why she had not been down to the marina. Noah and Carly let Simon in on the little secret—the boat.

Simon wanted to help, and they hoped Cappy wouldn't mind yet another kid coming into the yard. So off they went to Cappy's house.

Carly could talk a lot at times, so she filled Simon in on this new project of theirs. Before long, they arrived at Cappy's house and headed for the door, but it opened before they reached the top of the stairs.

Cappy just gave a look at Simon, shook his head, and said, "Let's get going."

Cappy and the kids started making their way to the old barn, pushing grass side to side as they struggled through the jungle that stood in their way. Cappy just stared for a bit, and everyone wondered what was wrong.

Cappy hadn't been out to the barn in fourteen years or so. The barn was in better shape than he had thought it would be—from the outside anyway. He pulled out an old set of rusty keys on a big ring. They looked a century old. Cappy grabbed the lock and went to open the barn. The kids couldn't wait to see what was in there! It seemed like years waiting for him to open that lock. After a bit of a struggle, they all heard a click, and it had opened. Cappy took the lock off and told Noah and the kids to swing the door open. They began to pull and pull. The door was stuck from not being used. They gave one big yank, and the door swung open as the kids went flying into the grass. Cappy started to laugh, probably for the first time in years. They all struggled back up, except for Noah.

"Let's get going," Carly said, but Noah just kept staring up in the air. Carly and Simon came over to Noah, and then Simon looked up, as well.

Noah had fallen under the bow of the boat—or should we say schooner. Both of the boys were speechless.

Carly had already sneaked a peek and didn't tell Noah how big this boat really was in detail. They had their own ship now. Noah turned and asked Cappy how in the world he got this here.

Cappy laughed and said, "Very carefully, my boy."

Cappy told them to take a walk down behind the shed, so they did. There was a road. They all looked at one another and began to walk down it. The road wasn't long, and it turned very sharply. When they made it to the turn in the road, they all stopped. Noah was smiling now—there was the ocean.

Carly, laughing now, said, "That's how they brought the big boat here. I can't believe Cappy's backyard is the ocean."

They ran back toward the barn when they heard an engine start up.

"Did you hear that?" asked Simon. Carly and Noah said that they had.

"Cappy has a tractor. Thank God," said Simon. "I thought we would have to cut all this grass by hand."

Cappy pulled the big tractor out of the barn and, boy, did that make their day. Noah couldn't believe how good things were going—he had friends and a boat!

Cappy swung the other door open, and the kids peeked in. They couldn't believe what they saw. There were three or four small sailboats hanging from the rafters that had never been in the water. The tools were placed very neatly in the spots where they belonged. Sails draped over beams, and wooden masts for the sailboats hung neatly from the giant walls of the workshop. One boat was still in the making at the rear of the barn—it looked like a skeleton.

Cappy started in on the grass with the tractor, and the kids did all the hard work by hand. Noah used a push lawn mower to get around the boat, and Carly and Simon cut all the grass surrounding the workshop with shears. Simon's hands were bleeding from the constant squeezing to cut the grass, but Carly was a driven one and didn't slow down. After two whole days and with the kids covered in dirt, they had finished. Cappy smiled. He hadn't seen the land in years.

The kids went home after a long day of work to return the next day and start the boat.

Noah was walking slowly after all that work and his mother had some clothes to do now, as well, seeing he was a walking mess. Noah opened the door, looking as if he had been trying to hog-tie a pig in a mud pit. Both the parents laughed. Noah could barely smile.

Noah's father asked him to come out back behind the house to see something. Noah walked slowly but steadily, and as he rounded the corner of the old house, he stopped. Noah was smiling now.

There were five gallons of paint and many brushes. This was great, but it got even better. In bags were used sandpaper and nails. In a large box, he found all the screws he would ever need. Noah was so happy. He had more than he would need to get started on the schooner.

His father smiled and told him, "Get some rest. You're going to need it." So he went upstairs and never made it to the shower. There was Noah—out like a light with his shoes still on his feet.

Morning came, and the kids banged on Noah's door, Carly ready to knock the thing down. Here came Noah, hair all a mess as he wobbled down the stairs from his room. They had brought a wagon to carry all the things Noah's dad had brought home for them. Noah managed to call Carly to tell her about all the things they had before he went up to his room. Well, she was ready, and Simon, with his hands wrapped up like a mummy from cutting the grass, trailed behind. The three were off and didn't want to be late.

After yet another long walk, they arrived at Cappy's house. He was all smiles seeing what they had brought. Cappy put them all sanding on one side of the boat, and he checked and replaced all the screws—called fasteners—on the planks of the boat. The kids worked for three days and looked red—like three cherries—from sanding the red paint off the bottom of the boat. But they had finished the job, and Cappy put them on the other side to do the same so that he could replace what was needed on the other side. Well, three more days went by and long hours until dark. They were finally done, for now at least. Both sides of the boat were ready for painting and refastening with new screws.

Cappy pulled up a chair and began to read. They all just looked at him, and he lifted his head and said, "Well, it won't paint itself."

So the kids went to town painting their new boat. Cappy seemed to think they put more paint on themselves than the boat, but they were trying. He knew they really wanted this, so he let them keep going. Four days later and three very run down kids from working such long hours. The kids could barely stand but they had finished the bottom of the boat, it looked like new. They were ready to start the topsides of the boat, but Cappy thought they needed to go take a break and be kids for a few days. So Cappy called all the shots—his word was the law. Carly wasn't happy about taking a break, but Simon, well, that was music to his ears.

Simon went home and stayed in bed for a few days, but Carly sneaked back on the boat and kept working on sanding the top side. As for Noah, his father had talked to his boss. The boss allowed Noah to come down to the yard and help his father, getting paid with things he needed instead of money.

After a few days, they all returned at the same time with

more supplies to finish the top side. They weren't looking forward to more sanding. When they saw Cappy standing on the top of the boat with his arms crossed looking down at the deck. There was a ladder from the barn laying against the boat. This wasn't a ladder Cappy would use seeing it was too small, someone had been there. They walked up and said, "Good morning, boss. We're ready to start the sanding." Simon's eyes rolled back into his head, dreading the thought.

"Well, Noah," Cappy said, "looks like the sanding fairy must have stopped by and done it for you." He looked toward Carly.

He had seen her up there from the house window now that the grass was gone. Carly looked down and thought she might have spoiled it for all of them.

Cappy said, "You remind me of someone, young lady."

Carly smiled and said, "Who would that be?"

"My wife," he said. "She never gave up." He smiled. "I'm glad you young people came into my life," he said.

Cappy had made a call while the kids finished the top side, knowing that the highest tide of the year was near and they would need that deep water to launch the big boat. His old friend Henry had a crane, and they would need him to come down to set the two large masts in place. That meant they needed to pull the schooner out with the tractor to the road where the crane could have the room to move around and place the masts on.

The schooner sat on a huge cradle with large steel wheels

to roll down to the water. So Cappy started to grease the old wheels to make sure they would roll without a problem. The kids cleared a path, making sure nothing was in the way, and they pulled the large boat all the way down to the water.

Simon couldn't wait to be able to use his charts on this boat, and Carly wanted to sail the big boat. Noah thought about how the boat would handle in the waters. He already thought like a captain. Carly had seen this in the way he sailed on her boat. This was going to be an interesting crew. They were all very different, but they worked well together—that's what made a great crew on a boat. Cappy could see, as well, that they worked as a team.

Cappy felt alive for the first time in many years, and Henry was so glad to hear that Cappy was making a move with a boat once again.

Cappy brought the tractor around, and the kids hooked up the big arm that was attached to the cradle to pull the boat. After they were done, Cappy hopped off the tractor to check it out and make sure they were good to go. It looked good, so Cappy, back on the tractor, now began to pull. The boat wiggled a bit but didn't move. He tried again with the tractor—smoking up a storm from trying to pull the huge boat. Finally, it began to move, and the kids jumped up and down, clapping away as Cappy headed for the dirt road that led to the beach ramp. They followed behind, smiling all the way, as the move was going well. Cappy stopped in a spot where Henry would be able to put the masts on without a problem and shut the tractor off. They all ran up to Cappy and hugged him at the same time. Cappy was so happy for them and himself.

The Big Launch

The next day, Simon and Carly were at Noah's house bright and early. They couldn't wait to get the boat in the water and sail it around to the other side of the island. They were eager to finish the work today. The launch would be tomorrow. After banging on Noah's door for a bit, he came out and was ready to go.

Carly said, "What takes you so long, anyway?"

"Well," Noah said, "I needed to think some things over in how we would get the boat around."

"What do you mean?" said Carly.

"There isn't going to be much wind. That could be a problem."

Carly told Noah, "You worry too much. Don't worry; there will be wind to fill her sails."

So off to Cappy's house they went. When they arrived, the crane was already there, and Cappy was hooking up the straps to lift the mast and boom up to the boat with the large crane. Cappy told Noah to stand on the other side and said,

"Tell Henry what I tell you." Henry couldn't see them from the crane.

After making sure all the straps were in place, Cappy gave the word to Noah telling Henry to start lifting the mast.

Cappy yelled to Simon and Carly, "Stand back!" He didn't want anyone getting hurt.

Up went the mast, and they relayed back and forth where Henry was to move to position the mast. Things were going well when, all of a sudden, they heard a bang. One of the straps had broken free, and the large hook was heading right for Cappy. He ducked and wrapped his hands around his head, ready for the hit. Carly ran in front of Cappy, right in the path of the flying hook. She put her hands up and gave deep stare toward the oncoming hook. They all could feel something in the air changing as Carly's eyes turned a bright emerald green. She pushed her hands forward as if there were something in her way, and the hook began to stop. Then she turned and guided the hook to the side very slowly.

Henry couldn't see from the crane, but he knew the strap was free.

The hook stopped and rested against the boat as Carly dropped to her knee and placed her hands on to the ground. Cappy, still ducking, began to turn his head and look at Carly. He had seen her eyes glow green and felt the power she possessed still in the air. He stood slowly as Henry came around to see if anyone had been hurt.

Cappy said, "Don't worry, Henry. Everything is good here."

Cappy started to hook the mast back up, glancing at Carly from time to time. Before long, they had put both masts in place, and the kids locked down the wires that held the mast up to the hull of the boat. Then, the boom and sails went up. Henry took his time after what had happened earlier, and they set the boom on one mast and the other boom on the forward mast. They were done for now but had to check everything well, seeing that the only things holding the masts up were the wires. This was very important and had to be done right. If not, when the wind filled her sails, the masts could fall right over. Cappy would check their work later to make sure.

Cappy went to thank his old friend Henry for coming down and putting the mast up. That was the least he could do, seeing they were short on money to pay the man. Henry wouldn't have a problem with Cappy being a little short. Henry was a longtime friend and wanted to help in any way he could.

After putting another ladder up, Cappy and all the kids checked everything one last time. Then, they climbed the mast, hooking up all the ropes to lift the sails. Cappy was getting tired, and he said, "Let's take a break and get some water. Sit for a bit." So they climbed off the boat and sat on the grass. Simon, still tired from sanding, laid on the ground. Noah couldn't stop looking at the large schooner they had brought back to life. No one said a word about what had happened yet, but looking off into the distance, Cappy did.

"Carly, I have seen one person who could do something like what you did earlier. I wanted to thank you for that."

Carly wondered who this was Cappy spoke of. Noah and Simon wondered, as well.

When Noah had gone to get the water from the back of the house, he noticed there was a clear path out the back door to the garden hose. There was another leading back to the other side of Cappy's house. He followed the path, leading him straight to a gravestone. It read, "Rest in peace, Sarah." Cappy had laid his wife to rest on his property so he could visit her all the time. There were flowers all around the big stone. Everything was kept beautiful in this hidden side of the yard. Noah hadn't said he had seen it, but Cappy was sure he had when he went back there.

Cappy told Carly there was something he wanted to show her and the others, but they must keep this secret to themselves and never tell anyone. They headed for the house, and Cappy opened the door for them all to come in. There were pictures all over the house of the boats he had built and of Cappy with his beautiful wife.

For a few seconds, Cappy studied Carly's face as he would an old treasure map. There was something about this girl Cappy couldn't put his finger on.

They went to the back of the house where there was a room that hadn't been touched since his wife had passed. They all went in, and Cappy opened a door that led to the attic. As they went up, they pushed all the cobwebs away. Once up there, Cappy headed to the end of the attic where he stopped and called Carly over. There was a big trunk with weird markings on it covered in dust.

Cappy turned toward Carly and asked, "Where are your parents were from?" as they looked down upon this old trunk.

She bowed her head and answered, "I was adopted by Mary, the woman I live with."

Carly was told by Mary that, years ago, a woman sailed in with two other men that looked as if they came from over a hundred years into the past. This woman came with a child. The woman had brought the child to the orphanage and told them she could not care for the child. She told them the child's name was Carly. Then, she left them with a letter. The letter was to go to the woman she asked them to seek out to care for this child. That woman's name was Mary.

Cappy's eyes widened. His wife had a sister named Mary.

As the woman said her good-bye to the little one, she cried and placed a locket on her.

Simon and Noah didn't know what to say.

Cappy said, "That's okay, child. My wife held the same powers you have, as well."

She looked up and smiled with relief after keeping this secret for so long. He asked to see the locket, so Carly pulled it out from her shirt, and Cappy's eyes widened as he turned white.

"That is what she had left you?"

"Yes," said Carly.

Cappy was barely able to speak. "My wife had the same locket," he said.

Cappy knew something he wasn't going to tell to this child at this moment. He just didn't know what to think. There was silence for a few moments as everyone tried to understand what was happening.

Cappy pulled out the old trunk and wiped the dust off. He told her to open it. Carly looked up at him as he nodded to open the trunk. Carly opened it as Noah and Simon tried to see from behind what was in the trunk. There were many things in this trunk—necklaces made of shells, paper with notes on them, and a handful of scrolls. But the thing that stood out the most was a big, very thick book, and the cover was made from leather of some sort. Carly picked up the dust-covered book and blew on it. Dust went flying, and she sneezed. As she opened the book, the boys tried to see what was in it, but the book was written in a very old way, and it would take time to figure out what it really said.

Cappy said to Carly, "This is yours now, young lady. Take care of it."

Cappy and the boys carried the trunk down the stairs and put it on their wagon to pull to Carly's house. Carly couldn't wait to be alone and try to figure out what it said. It was clear it would help her find out where she had come from.

Cappy told them go home and get some rest. Tomorrow was the big day. Henry was going to come by and drive the tractor so Cappy could be on the boat with the kids to take it around the island and back to the shipyard where Noah's dad worked. Noah's dad worked for a good friend of Cappy's. He was the man that worked on all the boats Cappy built when needed. So keeping the boat there wouldn't be a problem. It was far too large to go over to the mariner with the other small boats were Simon and Carly kept theirs.

The next day had finally come. They were all there so early that it was still dark out, but they didn't want to miss the tide, or they would never get the boat in the water until another very high tide came around—and that only happened twice a year.

Cappy had been working on the old engine in the boat here and there, but they wouldn't be able to use it to move the boat until they made it to the shipyard to get fuel. So the wind was their only hope.

Henry finally arrived, and they all climbed up on the boat. Henry took the ladder down, started the old tractor up, and off they went. It was a slow ride to the water. For Noah, it seemed like a lifetime, and Simon was worried something would go wrong before they could get there. Carly stretched out on the deck and enjoyed the ride. Before long, Henry was backing the tractor down to the water, and the boat was on its way in. They could feel the boat break free from the cradle and begin to float. All the kids were up and ready to raise the sails, but there wasn't any wind. This could be a problem. Simon kept telling Noah and Carly that they would never get out without some wind. Simon had been worried about this for days.

The boat began to drift off into the inlet, and they could be in trouble without the engine. Noah didn't show it, but he was worried. Cappy didn't seem worried at all. He seemed to keep an eye on Carly, watching to see if she was worried. He knew something the rest didn't.

With the boat finally in the water—and no wind—Henry stood by just in case they needed him. Simon, his head down and hands covering his forehead, repeated over and over, "I knew it." Noah tried to think of something to do before it was too late.

Cappy looked at Carly with a smile and said, "Well, young lady?"

"What is it, Cappy?" asked Carly.

I heard your boat was the fastest in the fleet at the marina. She smiled and went to the bow to lie down.

Noah and Simon said, "What on earth are you doing? Now's not the time to be lying down." But Cappy smiled as Carly put her hands in the air, and the sails began to fill. Before long, the old schooner was making her way out of the inlet. Cappy laughed. Noah and Simon were speechless, to say the least, and Noah knew this was going to come in handy someday—once again thinking like a captain. As they made the turn out of the inlet and started their long trip around the island, Simon gave a yell.

"What's wrong," said Noah.

"This boat has no name," yelled Simon.

Carly sat up, and before she could say a word, Cappy smiled and said, "Yes, it does, my boy."

They all hung on his words. "It is called the *Drifter*," he said as he laughed. Now with Noah at the helm and Carly pulling the lines tight for the sail, they made way for the island corner. Simon pulled out his chart and started setting a course. Cappy hadn't been out on the water in years. He stood on the bow and took in the fresh air.

Calm Before the Storm

There were some storm clouds ahead, and Noah wondered what kind of weather they were in for.

Before launching the boat, Cappy had stocked it up with canned goods and made sure the water tanks were full. You never know when you could need things like that. They were a few hours into the trip around the island, heading for the shipping channel, keeping some distance from the island. They could see many rocks on the beach as the *Drifter* plowed through the oncoming seas. So it was wise to keep a wide berth from the dangerous parts along the way. The wind had picked up now, and the sun was gone. You could see the Forbidden Islands in the distance. That seemed to bother Cappy. He didn't seem to want to look that way, but he couldn't help himself. Simon was down below checking the course of the boat on his charts, and Noah was steering. Meanwhile, Cappy and Carly made sure everything was tied down before encountering any heavy seas. There was no getting around that they were going to get caught in some weather.

The seas began to rise, and the schooner was throwing water over her bow as the *Drifter* fell off each oncoming sea. They could hear the hull creak as the ocean angered. Carly went down in the cabin for a break while getting some rain gear to stay dry. As she was down below dressing for the weather, she could see the *Drifter's* hull flexing in and out as the boat slammed off each growing wave.

Cappy didn't seem himself. He couldn't stop looking toward the Forbidden Islands. There was something he wasn't telling the young crew.

The storm became worse, and the rain came down like the sky had sprung a leak. They could hear the stress coming from the wires holding the mast up as the wind whistled through the sails. Cappy knew this was bad, and so did Carly. Noah thought they should take a sail down to relieve some of the stress upon the boat. Cappy agreed. Carly began letting one of the sails down. She could barely hold the rope lowering the sail as the wind became stronger. Just before losing the rope, Simon dived in to grab on with her. Cappy was trying to tuck the sail in as it came down, but all of a sudden, the wind gusted. Cappy went flying, and so did Carly and Simon. Cappy went right over the side, but he was still hanging onto the rail. Carly and Simon tried to get up, and Noah yelled to them to help Cappy. So the two worked their way over to the rail where Cappy was hanging on for dear life.

Drifter was flying right out of the water as Noah tried to keep her into the wind.

They couldn't get Cappy up. Now, the sail was flying straight off the side of the schooner and making the boat lay over. Finally, Carly had enough. Simon hung on for dear life as Carly's eyes began to turn green and light the whole deck up like a streetlight. Her arms up and a very angry face to boot, she gave Cappy a stare. Cappy began to rise and float though the air right back on the boat. Noah could not believe his eyes!

Simon was still hanging on as the *Drifter* listed on her side.

Carly put Cappy down to the deck as he just glared at her. Then, she whipped her hands and arms forward in front of her toward the loose sail. Slowly, the sail started to come in but went right back out. Noah thought she might not be strong enough for this.

Cappy raised his voice and yelled, "Carly, don't let that sail go! You're stronger than you could ever imagine!"

Carly became angry, and the whole boat was now surrounded by green light from the glow in her eyes. They couldn't look at her eyes without being blinded. The sail flew in, and to the deck it went. Carly dropped and laid there. She had passed out for a moment and then started to sit up. Simon and Cappy dived on the sail and tied it up to the rail before it took off again. By this time, with all that had happened, they found themselves just passing by the Forbidden Islands. There was no turning back. They all looked at one another. Cappy knew this could be a bad thing, but at least the boat was holding up. Little did he know that things were about to get worse.

In the distance, there was a flash of light. Cappy had seen this before. The ghost ship had come back, but they would be caught in the weather, as well. Cappy knew they needed to turn around and get back.

Noah yelled to Cappy, "When I tell you, turn the boat around and get us back away from the islands!"

Carly and Simon stood ready, waiting for the turn. The boom would swing, and they would have to duck quickly not to get hit.

Cappy yelled out, "Now! Now, Noah!"

The boat began to turn, and the boom swung wildly over their heads. Noah fought the wheel as the *Drifter* laid into the turn. If he were to let go of the wheel, it could spin and break his arm. Noah held the wheel tightly as they retied all the lines holding the boom to head the other way. Finally, Noah turned the wheel slowly to straighten the boat. They were heading for the corner of the island with the hope they had water deep enough to pass that close. In the distance, they could see the big ship heading their way.

Simon began yelling, "They're gaining on us!"

Cappy knew this wasn't good and that the other ship would catch up. Noah was holding his own, keeping the boat steady for a close pass to the island.

Looking at Carly, Cappy said, "It's up to you now. You're our only hope."

Carly bowed to one knee, and her eyes lit up again. Cappy was sure the ship's crew could see the light from her eyes in the near distance, and their wizard, as well. Carly pushed forward with her hands and filled the one sail with as much wind as it could take. The boat was really moving now, but the mast was creaking with all the pressure on one sail. But the ship was close enough now to see the captain and their wizard. Things were going to get ugly very quickly.

The wizard had his hands in the air. Simon saw this before with Carly. Simon had a bad feeling that trouble was coming soon.

He yelled to Carly, "That wizard is starting to look like you—but with a *red* glow!"

Simon quickly dropped to the deck. Carly whipped around, mad as one could be, and threw her hand toward the large ship. Their sails, once full of wind, were turned and pushed the other way by a thundering blast of energy flying out from Carly's hands. Then, with one wave of her arm to the left, the whole ship turned, and all the crew went flying to the side as the mighty vessel laid right over. One could see this very well now that they were right on the stern of the *Drifter*. The wizard fell back, just to get back up and look Carly right in her eyes. He knew this girl had very strong powers. Their ship still turning with Carly angered as could be, the two staring each other down. This wasn't over. Carly wanted a piece of that old wizard, and he knew it.

The islands were close, and the *Drifter* started passing the last island. They felt a bump, but the schooner kept going. Then, they all heard a yell from the captain. "This is not over, Cappy. I knew we would meet again!" But the *Drifter* was back in safe waters, and it started to calm down a bit as they headed toward the mainland. Noah asked Cappy what that was all about. How did he know that it was Cappy on this boat? Carly, exhausted, sat on the deck with her head down. Simon tried to catch a breath. They knew Cappy had some explaining to do.

With things calming down now, Simon went down below to find a course for Noah to steer. Simon came up and told Noah, "We need to head north ten degrees, and that should lead us to the harbor inlet."

Noah looked at Simon and asked, "What do you mean that it *should?*"

"Sorry. I meant that it *will.*" Simon looked worn out from all that had happened.

Carly looked at Cappy, and she just had to ask. "What haven't you told us? How did that captain know you?"

He looked down and said, "My wife didn't pass. That was Captain Black and his ship, *Dark Spirit*. He is the meanest pirate ever to sail the ocean." Cappy had many questions to answer now.

Black was a tall but bulky man who wore his pistol on the leather belt holding up his pants. His long, black hair fell from under the leather hat upon his head, shadowing brown eyes with no soul. His wizard called Ile, he is the one they speak of in Silver Shell.

Carly knew of this Ile—it was her great-grandfather's name according to all the stories being told. Once again, being adopted, nothing made sense.

"My wife and I had been in a storm once before. We went beyond the Forbidden Islands, as well. That's where we met

Captain Black. The wizard had never seen powers like those my wife Sarah possessed. We were adrift without sails due to the storm, and that's how they caught us. Sarah fought back, but the wizard was too strong for her. The captain promised to have the wizard vanish me if Sarah did not go with them. So Sarah went to save my life. She made me promise the captain never to return to the Forbidden Islands, for that was their place, not to be traveled by any other. For this, he would not harm Sarah. The wizard wanted to learn more from her and possibly turn her to stand by his side. The wizard spoke a few words, and the ship vanished. I fixed one of the sails on the *Drifter* and went home, never to see the ocean again until now."

Cappy looked at Carly and softly spoke, "You are much more powerful than Sarah was, and you have proven to be some match for that wizard without knowing how to harness what you have. The wizard knows this, and he knows if you learn the way your powers work, he would be no match for you."

"There is something else," said Cappy. "That woman that brought you to the orphanage was Sarah. Mary is her sister. I didn't know she was to have a child."

Carly looked at Cappy and exclaimed, "This would mean you're my father!"

"Well, let's not get our hopes too high yet!" Cappy smiled with joy, and Carly ran to hug him.

Noah listened while he watched the course closely. Simon, well, he just didn't know what to say, but he was happy for Carly. Simon went to check the course after an hour and made some corrections for Noah to follow. Carly was sleeping on Cappy's lap. It wasn't long before they could see the light of the town glaring in the distance. Boy, that was a great sight to see! They would all have a lot to talk about when they reached home.

Hours later, the sun began to rise, and the orange glow filled the sky. They were nearing the inlet to the harbor. Simon tried to fix what he could on the way in, but the *Drifter* was some mess. They would have a lot of work to do after that storm and the run-in with Captain Black and the wizard named Ile. Noah's parents would be waiting at the dock after not coming home the night before.

Simon went down below to wake Carly and Cappy before they reached the dock. Now being light, you could see all the damage. *Drifter* was worse than Simon thought.

They all dragged out the dock lines to get ready to tie the old girl up across from the marina. Noah brought the boat in very gently like he had been doing this for years. The people on the dock, including his father, could see this. The first line was thrown on the dock. They slipped it over one of the poles on the pier as Carly pulled it in tight and then tied it firmly to the *Drifter*. Then, Cappy and Simon did the same. The beaten-down boat was safely at the pier.

Noah's mother ran to him, hugging like she had not seen him in years. His father just looked at him. He knew his son was born to be on the ocean. They would go home and get some rest. Cappy shook Noah's father's hand. Just the look Cappy had in his eyes was enough to tell Noah's father what he thought of his son.

Carly looked lost. She had many things on her mind. Just then, Mary walked from the crowd, her long, dark hair being blown by the wind. Mary looked at Carly with her deep green eyes. Carly looked at her, barely keeping her eyes open.

Carly asked, "Who is my mother?"

Mary looked at Cappy and then turned back to Carly, saying, "We will talk later."

Mary yelled to Cappy as he walked down the pier. Cappy turned. There was a moment of silence as he looked at this short, thin woman he hadn't seen in many years. Finally, the silence broke when Mary asked Cappy to stop in tomorrow because they needed to talk. Mary knew she had much to say to them, and some things were not going to go well after keeping Sarah's secret.

Cappy gave a nod and said, "I look forward to the visit." Mary smiled.

Noah went home with his mom and dad. As they walked in the door of the house, his mom went right to the kitchen to cook something up. Noah and his father went out on the porch to talk. His dad sat down and just looked at his son, and then Noah's began to talk. He told his father everything. At the same time, the father could hear in Noah's voice this wasn't over. The boy became a man in his father's eyes as he spoke, the words of a true friend to his shipmates and without so many words he told him he would be helping Carly. Noah told his father that Carly was not the type of person to leave this whole thing behind her. Carly would go out there to search for the answers she needed with her own boat. Noah knew that she would need the *Drifter* and its crew to take on that so-called ghost ship. Noah's dad knew he would be going out to take on the legend of the ghost ship, but there would be nothing he could do to stop Noah from helping his friend. His father stood up and put his arm around the man his son had become and went in to have dinner.

Cappy was home looking at all the old photos of himself and Sarah. He wouldn't sleep that night. He thought of what Mary had to say for keeping this child a secret from him.

Simon was happy to be home and passed out on his bed. They would have to come drag him out in the morning. The day was over with so many unanswered questions, to all.

No More Secrets

The next morning, Carly was up early. She wanted answers. Out of bed, she flew down the stairs to see Mary, her aunt.

"Can we talk?" asked Carly.

Mary looked at her and bowed her head. "Please wait until Cappy gets here. That would be better."

Carly ran up to her room, not very happy with having to wait even longer. She pulled the big book of magic from under her bed. *This holds the answers to my life*, she thought to herself. So she began to read more closely, but the book was very hard for this young girl to understand.

Meanwhile, Noah woke, as well, and he was out the door in no time before anyone could catch him. Off to Simon's he went. Upon arriving at Simon's house, he found Simon sound asleep and still wearing his shoes. Simon's room was a mess—he had sails to his boat in one corner and a pile of chart books in the other. What Noah did like about this room was the charts all over the walls like posters. Simon was all about the ocean, for sure. With a shake, he woke Simon up from a dream. Simon jumped up, yelling, "Duck!"

Noah laughed and said, "What are you talking about? Get it together. We need to go be there for Carly when this talk starts."

Cappy had already started heading to Mary's for this talk. He hadn't slept a wink the night before. Like Carly, he wanted to know why this had to be a secret. Now, Cappy hadn't been to Mary's house in over fourteen years—since his wife had been gone. It wouldn't be easy for Cappy walking into the past.

Well, everyone arrived at Carly's house at about the same time. Simon looked like a mess, but that was nothing new. Mary had been making coffee. They all could smell the brew on the way up the sidewalk. She greeted them at the side door. The kitchen was right there. One by one, they made their way over to the big, oval dinner table that was surrounded by chairs.

Cappy walked in very slowly. It had been years since he had seen this house. Nothing had changed. As he walked across the hardwood floor that still creaked like years ago, Cappy could not take his eyes of the picture hanging on the wall of Sarah and Mary. He was the last one to pull a chair out at this table. He spent many holidays at this table with Sarah. Cappy was having a very hard time dealing with all of this.

Carly came down the stairs, surprised to see all her friends there for her. Cappy watched Carly as she came down. Now that they were all sitting, Mary turned to start pouring coffee when she slammed the cup on the counter. She stood for a moment.

"You know what? Forget the coffee," Mary lashed out.

"Enough is enough. Let's get to it!" She pulled out a chair and sat at the table. Mary was a blunt woman. She had held this in for too long. She looked at Carly and said, "I won't tell you what you already know. The rumor is true of the woman that came to town with a child. That child was you, Carly. The orphanage sought me out to care for this child, as you all know. Secrets. I am tired of them!"

Sarah had come back not only with a child there was a letter for Mary. Sarah's letter told Mary that the captain and Ile would not harm Cappy or the child if Sarah remained with them. They would jump through time, taking what they wanted from others and hiding everything on an island. Sarah agreed to do as they'd asked. Cappy wasn't told everything. He did not know of this child she was carrying. Sarah thought he might try to save them. With Sarah expecting a child, she would not have been able to save Cappy if he'd tried.

Mary looked at Carly and Cappy and then walked over to her desk. It was locked. Carly always wondered what lay inside of that one drawer. As she opened the desk, you could hear a pin drop. She walked over to Carly and handed her a letter, and she handed another to Cappy. There had been two other letters Mary had been holding. The letter had much to say to Carly and about the book Cappy had given her. Cappy reading with tears in his eyes of hurt and pain, but much anger was within him, as well. He had missed his child growing up—this made Cappy angry.

Mary had everyone get up to move the table and pulled the rug back from where it stood for so many years. With a knife, she popped the floorboard up and placed it to the side. There, under the floor, hidden for years, was a staff made from some rare wood that Cappy had never seen. At the top of the staff was a jewel. Mary picked it up and handed it to Carly. As soon as she touched the wooden staff, the jewel lit up.

"This was your mother's, and now it's yours," Mary said, smiling.

Noah and Simon looked very worried of what was to come.

"Your mother told me to put it in a safe place long before she was taken," Mary said. Carly was speechless. Mary knew the power it held to the one that knew how to use this.

Mary gave a sigh and said, "I know you will chase them down to reach your mother. That is why I have given you this. You will need it. First, you must learn the book to understand what you hold."

Noah stood and said, "I'm in. Let's go after Ile and his ship, *Dark Spirit*."

"This is not your fight," said Cappy.

Simon stood quickly to look Cappy in his eyes. "It is now," he said.

Carly asked why she didn't use her powers to fight, but Mary had made a vow not to use them as a child, she did play with them when no one was around.

Noah spoke out, "Well, that's done. We go together or not at all."

Cappy stood and paused for a moment before he spoke. He looked at all the brave, young people in the room and began to smile.

"Well, crew, we have much to fix before we can go after that ship, and we need something to protect the boat since they have cannons," said Cappy. He would work on that with Simon. "Let's all go home for the day and meet at the *Drifter* in the morning."

Cappy walked over to Mary to thank her for taking very good care of the child, then he turned toward Carly and winked with a smile. She ran over and hugged Cappy. They held each other for some time. Then, Cappy told Carly to get on the book.

"We need you. I need you, my daughter," he said. Carly smiled and headed upstairs. Her life was finally starting to make sense. As they all left the house, you could see they were all thinking of what was to come. Would they be able to pull off attacking the pirate ship? Well, they were sure going to try.

Rebuilding the *Drifter*

Morning came, and Noah crawled out of bed, being a bit sore from the storm. He threw some clothes on and flew down the stairs to get a head start. He was going to wake the sleeping dead—Simon, that is. On his way out the door, his mom caught him for a quick talk—or so he thought. Noah sat, and Mom did the talking.

She said to him, "I never chased my dreams, but I am very happy the way life turned out raising you."

Noah had never had this kind of talk with his mom. He knew it was for a reason.

"Noah," she said, "we both know you were never one to have many friends for some reason, but the ones you have seem to be special. I want you to do what is in your heart. I know your dad is worried, and so am I."

Noah, lost for words, had never seen this side of his mother.

"You need to finish what you have started, or you will wonder for the rest of your life. Your great-great-grandfather was a sailor, as well."

Noah didn't know of this. "Why didn't you tell me?" asked Noah.

Noah's mother just looked at him before answering. "There was a reason I didn't tell you this. He was lost at sea, but he didn't go very far when this had happened. He was a whale-boat captain. I could see in you what my grandmother had told me of him and his ways. I didn't want the same to happen to you," his mother said softly.

Noah's mother had a sea trunk from great-grandfather's early years, full of everything he started with as a young lad being a sailor. She stood up and told him to come with her. Noah followed.

In the cellar of the house was a corner full of all his mom's things. Within the big pile of memories, there was a trunk, old and full of dust. They carefully pulled it out and wiped off all the dust. Noah couldn't wait any longer. What was in this box?

Mom had a very old key that would open the past of her family lying in this box. She placed the key in the old lock and turned it. Nothing happened. She tried again, and there was a pop. It had opened. After pulling off the lock, they looked at each other.

Noah's mother had never looked inside. "I should have done this long ago," she said.

Slowly, they opened the chest of time. It was like new inside, both of their eyes wide as to all the things he had left behind. The first thing Noah saw was a gold compass— still slightly shiny—one that could be held within his hand. He found different things like charts and tools to navigate with, as well. A very old ink pen would be in a box near a set of books, the books being this man's logs he would write in. There were other small treasures that his great-great-grandfather had picked up along the way. There was one thing Mom had seen before. She reached in to pick up a necklace with a gold medallion hanging from a leather strap.

"Noah, my grandmother showed me this in a photo a very long time ago," she said. "Your great-great-grandfather never left it behind, and he never took it off, either."

Why did he leave this behind? Noah began to think there was more to this story, but what?

Mom went upstairs, and Noah carried the box to his room, placing it gently on the floor to look through later. He took one last look before he left. He reached in, picked up the medallion, and put it on. He stood for a moment, and then off to Simon's he went. Now, Noah had questions of his own, but he needed to get going on fixing the *Drifter*. This would have to wait.

Noah went to pick Simon up, and sure enough, Simon was in bed again.

"Simon!" Noah yelled. "We need to meet Cappy and Carly down at the boat. Wake up, for God's sake!"

Simon dragged himself out of bed. Boy, he really needed to clean himself up. They set out for the dock. The whole town had heard what had happened. It was a small town to begin with.

When they arrived at the boat, there were supplies sitting in front of the *Drifter* on the pier. Someone had stacked a big pile of new wood and three new sails that looked like they would fit the *Drifter*. That was not all that sat on the pier—there were tools and even food to stock the boat. They just looked at one another. Maybe Cappy brought all of this? Just then, Cappy walked up with Carly. Cappy took a good look and smiled.

"Wasn't me, but we sure need all of it, that's for sure."

"If not you, Cappy, then who?" asked Noah.

Noah's dad came walking over since he was at work in the same shipyard. "Well, Noah, it seems the town wants to know what's out there, as well. They have been dropping things off here all morning. No one has ever escaped the legendary ghost ship, but you have."

The shipyard carpenters came down with their tools, and the sailmaker did, as well, along with Noah's dad's boss. The boss told the men to get to work putting the boat back together.

Noah turned to his father with a big smile, and Cappy grinned. "What we are standing here for?" Cappy asked. "Let's do this."

The mast was taken off with the yard's crane and laid beside the damaged boom on the pier. There, they could work on the rigging for the *Drifter*. Cappy, Noah, and the rest of the crew began fixing the boat, now having everything they needed and more. Simon went below to build a bigger chart table for his charts, and Carly was up on the other boom that had held up in the storm, replacing all the lines for the sails—just to make sure they wouldn't have any problems. Cappy was fastening everything that had loosened up around the deck of the boat, and there were a lot of screws going in that boat after what she had been through. Noah jumped on the dock to help the men repair the mast and boom. Where they were going, Noah needed to know as much as he could. Seeing they were going to pick a fight with a ship much larger than theirs, they needed to be in top shape to survive this voyage.

Cappy yelled over to the pier, "Noah, tighten the stay wires that hold the mast up! We wouldn't want that to come crashing down!"

The day was hot and long. They had accomplished a lot of things but had a ways to go. So they decided to call it a day.

Cappy said, "Same time in the morning. Okay, crew?" Then, off they went, heading home at last.

Carly went home to learn the book and about the staff she had been given. She ran all the way home, flew in the house, and grabbed her staff, eager to master the power it held. You could hear her out in the backyard cursing as she tried to make the piece of wood work. Just then, to her great surprise, Mary came out to help her. She did know a little about this. Carly picked up the staff and repeated the words she was able to read in the book—but there was nothing but a small glow of the jewel. Carly was ready to pull her hair out.

"It must be broken. Why won't it work?" Carly asked.

Mary asked to see the staff. Her eyes began to glow, and with a few words and anger in her eyes, the staff fired a green stream of powerful light and energy that hit a large tree. They heard the wood cracking. Carly looked at Mary, and then they both ran as the tree began to fall. Carly and Mary jumped over into the bushes as it hit the ground—one bounce, and then it stopped. They looked at each other, full of grass and dirt, hair everywhere.

Mary smiled. "Well, Carly, it has been years since I played this game. Guess I overdid it, wouldn't you say?"

Carly laughed. "You lied to me a bit."

It seemed Mary knew more than she chose to show or tell anyone. But Carly was happy she would have some help. Mary told her, "There is much in that book of our ancestors I just don't understand, but we will study it together. Enough with the staff for now. Let's work on controlling what you have inside." Covered in dirt and grass, they headed for the house.

Cappy, at home making something to eat, could not stop thinking that Sarah was still out there and about this daughter he was never told of. He was angry and happy at the same time. He had not slept for days, so off to bed Cappy went. He really needed an early night.

Now, Simon, on the other hand, had brought some of the supplies home. He wanted to make some sort of weapon against the pirate ship. He broke out the sketching table and began to draw what seemed to be a huge slingshot to fire something at the ship. He spent all night working on how it could work and where to put it. After hours of working on this project, he had it down. But they would have to build two for each side of the boat and one for the bow and stern to protect the entire boat.

This big rubber band would throw any sort of object—anything from a rock to a watermelon. But coal would be the thing to use. If they could get the coal to light on fire, it would be hard to put out on the ghost ship. We will work on that tomorrow, he thought to himself. Simon smiled. He'd just found a way to fight back. Wait until the others see this. So off to bed he went, thinking of what he had to show his friends in the morning.

They all met up at the dock in the morning, Simon showing Cappy the blueprints to his secret weapon. Cappy smiled. He told Simon, "We will get working on this right away."

Noah was working on the mast and boom. With the help from the men in the shipyard, they were getting closer to finishing.

Noah had met a young man who wanted to sail with them on this hunt for the ghost ship. His name was Hunter—how fitting. He was a very big young man with the strength of two men. Noah thought this could be good for what they had to face. Hunter would be going, as well.

The crane showed up to place the mast back on. Hunter was good with fixing that kind of thing, so he would be helpful in many ways in the future, Noah thought. The crane placed the mast into the deck as everyone else grabbed the wires to hold it up. They began to fasten the wires and tighten them down all around the rails. Next was the boom. The crane swung it over and held it in place as the crew secured it tightly to the mast before letting it go. Once again, the *Drifter* had both masts standing tall and looking better than ever. Hunter and Noah put everything back together when the crane was clear from the *Drifter*. Cappy and Simon were mounting the ship's so-called cannons, all six of them. They hoped that there would be enough, but only time would tell.

There was a holding compartment within the schooner's hull, where the coal was stored. The coal truck headed for the *Drifter*. When the truck was close enough, the man dumped a big pile of coal. Hunter and Noah began filling the holding compartment with all the coal. Carly was sitting on the dock studying the book. They left her alone, seeing she had to learn as much as she could. Cappy and Simon stocked the boat with the food and supplies they needed. The time was getting close. Soon, they would all meet to discuss a plan. After all, they needed something.

After five more days of backbreaking work, the boat was ready to sail. They had finally finished. *Drifter* would have never gone back together so fast without the help from the townspeople. Noah went over to see his dad standing by his boss who had helped them so much.

Noah shook the boss's hand and said, "Thank you."

The boss looked at the young man for a moment and said, "Son, you're a brave one. Your father should be proud of you, chasing down a mighty ghost ship. No other has been brave enough to try."

The boss didn't know of many things—like Carly's mother being on the ship and the wizard's deal with Cappy. Nonetheless, taking on something everyone feared was more than enough for him. They all went home for a few days off before the big meeting. They needed a plan in order to take on such a ship. Saving Carly's mother from the wizard would be no easy task.

The Big Plan of Attack

A few days went by, and it was time for the meeting of the minds at Cappy's house. One by one, the whole crew showed up, including Hunter.

As they stood on the porch, Noah gave a knock. Cappy opened the door with a grin. They all had come. Cappy sat in his chair, and the kids sat on the floor and listened.

Simon had been studying all the Forbidden Islands and how deep the water was in certain places. He had checked for anything they could use to get away—if needed—or surprise them. He showed Cappy all of what he had found. Simon was the first to speak—so much for the listening part. He thought it would be good to wait for a day when the tide was high at dawn to hug the islands. This way, they could not be noticed right away. But Noah thought it would be better to do this as the sun went down and sneak up on the ghost ship and board the boat.

Now, Carly made it clear she wanted on that ship. "Low or high, we're going! I have a bone to pick with that wizard!" she snarled.

Cappy had to agree with Noah, but how would they know the ship was there? The plan would have to catch the pirates off guard, or how could they get on to save Sarah?

Cappy listened to them argue over what would work better. After a long time of debate, Cappy yelled out, "Enough! We will do this at dawn. There is no way of getting around the wizard knowing."

After thinking about this, Noah knew Simon was right. They would have to take them on, head-on.

Cappy told Hunter to get all the lamp oil he could find in town. They would use this to soak the coal and light it on fire. The pirates would have their hands full putting the coal out so their boat didn't burn down. Maybe that would give them the time they needed.

Cappy said, "Now, Carly, how far have you come with the book? The staff took a tree down, but will it take the mast of that ship down?"

Carly said, "I guess we will have to find out, won't we?"

Cappy smiled and said to Noah, "Noah, I want you and Hunter to keep the boat tight to the ship. We need time to find Sarah."

"What about the pirates?" Noah asked.

"What about them? You have Hunter to keep them off the boat." Cappy laughed at the thought. "I'm sure you two will be fine."

Simon just shook his head, talking to himself. "Glad he thinks it's funny."

Cappy was trying very hard not to show how worried he really was. He didn't want the kids to know. He knew this was no time to be laughing.

"Now, Carly, you go home and get back to that book. There must be something we can use in there," said Cappy. He turned to Noah and said, "You look for as many hooks as you can find. This way, we can throw them up over the rails of the ship and climb the rope attached to them to get us aboard."

Now, everyone had something to do. They all left Cappy's house to find what they would need to be ready, come the first day of high water at dawn. Cappy sat back down and reached over to grab a photo of Sarah. He held it in his hands, staring with anger. He knew this had to be done for Carly more than anything. Cappy also knew her friends would stand by her to the end. This was a rare bunch—a handful of personalities that would work in their favor. He worried about Carly and the powers she held, he was more worried how far the wizard would go to stop her. Cappy knew they all would have their hands full with this adventure.

On the way home, Noah had a talk with Carly. He was worried how far she would go to deal with this wizard. Would she put them in jeopardy? So as they walked, Noah voiced his concerns. Carly stopped at one point and looked at Noah with hurt in her eyes. She snapped, "I need to know where I came from ... why this happened."

Carly promised Noah that she would not put any of them

in harm's way and that she would stop if Noah told her to back down.

Noah looked her in the eyes with a deep stare. "There's a good chance we will have to face Ile and Black face-to-face," said Noah.

She quickly answered, "Let's hope not—for his sake." Noah felt trouble coming, and he hoped that she kept her promise.

Noah dropped Carly off and headed for home. They would take the *Drifter* for a test run the next day, testing the new cannons that Simon had invented for the boat. Simon had much imagination, which was good when you don't have much to work with.

The next morning, they all showed up. Simon late with a handful of papers and charts, dropping them everywhere, Hunter would give him a hand getting all his things on the boat. It seemed that Hunter was taking Simon under his wing. After fueling up the boat, Cappy gave the go-ahead for Noah to take the *Drifter* of the dock. He did so very gently. All the dockworkers watched as they left. Once out of the harbor, the crew tested the cannons.

Simon designed them with two pieces of wood going straight up and down and two pieces going along the deck of the boat. Then, a board was placed between the upright wood like a ramp that could be adjusted to go up and down. That would allow the coal to fly high in the air or give a straighter shot if needed. He used rubber bands attached to the wood going up and down, one on each side, Then in the middle of the bands would be a piece of leather, like a big patch, the leather wouldn't catch on fire and would hold the coal as it flew up the ramp and though the air. At the bottom of this ramp would be a hole to stick a pin or nail that held the rubber bands back. When they pulled the pin to release the bands, the coal would be picked up as it took off with great power like a big slingshot.

Now out of the harbor, Noah told Hunter and Simon to get some coal and lamp oil. They would fire this oversized slingshot to see how far it would go. Simon and Hunter loaded the cannon after pulling back the band and making good and sure the pin was in place, so this didn't take off on its own. Hunter placed the coal on the ramp right in front of the rubber band and leather patch, now it was ready.

Noah gave the command. "Light it, and let the coal fly."

Hunter lit the coal, and Simon pulled the pin—off like a cannon, the coal went flying through the air as far as the eye could see.

"Flying fire!" Noah yelled with a laugh. "Let's see how they're going to like this."

So after a few more, Noah put the boat into a turn and whipped it around a bit. The crew tried to keep up without getting hit by the boom swinging from side to side. Simon diving so he didn't get hit but as Hunter was laughing so hard he did, off the boat and into the water He went. Noah slowed the boat and then turned to get Hunter—who was laughing, to Noah's surprise.

"Good thing we have this guy," said Cappy. He was laughing along with everyone else.

Still in the water and looking up, Hunter said, "Guys, now would be a good time to get me out, don't you think?"

They swung the boom over and lowered a line that would run though a pulley with a hook on the end, than they all pulled, up come hunter back on the boat. Simon in stitches, this was so funny until Hunter threw him in the water. Now they were all laughing as they pulled Simon out as well, Simon really need a bath anyway.

"That's enough for one day!" shouted Noah. "Let's head to the dock."

After getting the boat back in and tied safely to the dock, they all went home, but before that, Simon broke the news that they had three days. They all turned and looked as Simon as their smiles vanished.

"What do you mean *three days*, Simon?" said Noah.

"That's the next high water," mumbled Simon.

With that in mind, they all went home. It was time.

The Hunt Begins

The second day came, and the kids packed their bags for more than they could ever imagine. They would be leaving at midnight. It would take hours to make it to the Forbidden Islands. Noah was hoping this would go well, after the last time they seen the wizard he knew this would be no easy task. Carly had fire in her eyes—she wanted more answers to what had happened. Why would her great-grandfather turn on his own family like this? He made it clear he was going to give Carly a fight, and little did he know, that's just what she wanted. With her staff in hand, she headed out the door.

Now, Cappy was really worried about how Carly would react to all of this—particularly meeting her mother. Carly had much anger in her. Could he keep her under control with her powers? Noah and Simon worried about the same, but Carly was their friend, and they would stand by her to the end. Hunter was like a lost soul with a new family, and nothing would stand in the way of that with him. Hunter was a foster child at one time, but he didn't really have anyone until now. This was a powerful crew of young people, all with their own dreams. But nonetheless, they were there for each other first and foremost.

Cappy showed up at the boat first. He sat down, looking out toward the Forbidden Islands. He knew this was going to be a trip where many things could go wrong. Cappy worried for the kids, but he knew they were going with or without him. So he needed to go—he had faced this once before. Would Sarah be angry with him for going against her wishes and bringing Carly out to face a dangerous wizard?

The *Drifter's* crew showed up, looking like they hadn't slept since they'd last been at the boat. One by one, they came aboard. Simon went down below to catch the seabags with all their clothes. Every bag bounced off Simon's head. The whole crew began to laugh. There were bunks for all of them. They weren't big, but they all could manage. Hunter, on the other hand, might be sleeping on the deck—he was a big guy, much bigger than the bunks. They went down to unpack and claim their spots. Soon after, they all made their way up to the deck where Cappy was waiting for them.

Noah told Hunter to fire the engine up, and Simon and Carly were ready to throw the lines holding the boat tied to the pier. Hunter came up and sent Simon on the dock to take the lines of the pier. They needed one person on the dock to do this. Noah gave the word, and the lines were untied and pulled to the boat. Simon jumped on, nearly falling in the water. The boat backed down as Noah turned the wheel hard over. Just then, he put the throttle in forward, and they were on the way out.

As Noah headed for the channel markers, the crew put all the dock lines away. They all looked back at the small town as it became farther away, almost like they would never see home again. There was a chill in the air that sent goose bumps up

Noah's neck. He didn't say much, but by the look on his face, he didn't have to. Hunter and Carly pulled the forward sail up. It took a moment, but she filled with wind. Hunter shut the engine down now that they were under sail power. Wind or not, they had Carly for that.

Carly sat on the bow, looking down as the waves curled up the bow. Cappy went up to talk to her, but Carly wasn't in a talking mood. Cappy looked back at Noah. He was worried.

Simon was tangled up in a swarm of charts, glasses all sideways and looking like a mess. Hunter helped him pick everything up. He was worried, as well.

Hunter looked at Simon and said, "My friend, you have me. There is nothing to fear." Simon and Hunter laughed.

Well, you couldn't see the lights of the town anymore, and Noah was looking at Simon for a new course to pass through the Forbidden Islands. They still had hours to go, but Simon needed to get this course right, or they would run aground and beach the boat. Simon was working on this, checking everything twice to make sure. He had charts everywhere. Simon yelled out a new course to Noah, this would bring them through the shallow water in a few hours. After passing there, it would only be a matter of time before they had their hands full.

The sun began to rise earlier than they'd hoped for. The wizard would see them coming. There would be nothing they could do about that. Noah gave the order to start soaking the coal for the cannons. They would take on Black's ship head-on. Before long, the sun rose, and there would be no surprise for the pirate boat and its wizard.

Drifter was about an hour away, and they could see the fog rolling in. Maybe there was hope yet? The fog could work in their favor to sneak up on old Captain Black.

Simon and Carly set up tubs of coal and lamp oil on each side of the boat. Now with three coal tubs full and soaking ready to go they could only wait. The fog became thicker as they came closer to the island. They would be passing without even seeing the island with such thick fog.

Simon yelled up, "Noah, we should be coming up on the shallow water in moments!"

Just then, they felt a bump. Noah was too close. Then, the felt another bump. The boat was hitting bottom. Noah quickly turned the boat to deeper water. After one last bump, they were doing better. Carly looked down in the water. She could see the bottom, crabs walking around and all. She knew that wasn't a good thing, but they pushed on. This went on for at least a half hour before they got out of the shoals. After a stressful half hour, they were clear and looking for the wizard. But the fog was so thick that they could not see a thing.

Noah yelled out, "Carly! Hunter! Lower the sail!"

They would run on the engine slowly so they didn't hit another boat, pirate boat that is.

Cappy stood on the bow, looking, and Simon stood by Noah. There was silence between all of them like the calm before a storm. Time passed, and the fog began to lift. Soon, they would have no place to hide. Noah slowed the boat down to a creep, and Hunter could see something. He pointed off the side of the boat. There was what looked to be a boat off to the side of them. Just then, there was a loud crash, and wood broke as they all fell to the deck of the *Drifter*.

"Wrong boat!" Noah yelled.

They had hit the *Dark Spirit*, Captain Black's ship. All they heard was the *Drifter* being ripped apart. There was yelling on the pirate boat to get up on deck.

Noah saw that their sails were still up. Looking at Carly and Hunter, he yelled, "Fire! Fire the cannons at their sails!"

Simon frantically tried to light the coals, saying to himself, "Light! Come on, light!"

Noah yelled, "Simon, now what are you waiting for?" Just then, the coal lit right up, and Simon ran around lighting the rest of the coal tubs.

Cappy had fallen and was hurt.

Carly yelled to Cappy, "Stay down!"

Noah turned the *Drifter* away from the ship, as the *Drifter* came about to face her fight the cannons on the *Drifter* would launch their fireballs at the sails on *Dark Spirit*. Simon ran back and forth to each cannon as Carly and Hunter fired over and over. The sails were burning, and the deck burned, as well. You could see Captain Black yelling at the crew to put the fire out. Just then, they fired a shot at the *Drifter*, taking the top of the mast right off. Noah headed right for the ship as the kids kept firing flying fireballs of coal all over Black's ship. Before they could get alongside of the pirate ship, the wizard walked across the deck. His arms and hands went up as his eyes began to glow. Carly knew they were in trouble. She ran for her staff, but just as she was able to grab it, the wizard hit Cappy with a blast of energy that flew from his hands. Cappy was already hurt, but now he was just lying on deck. What Noah and Cappy feared the most was about to come.

How powerful could Carly possibly be? thought the wizard. He was about to find out. Carly stood up, looking at him face-to-face with her staff in one hand and his staff in his hand.

Ile looked at Carly and laughed. "Do you really think you're powerful enough to stop me, child?" He laughed even harder.

"*Child*! Who you calling a child, old man? Enough talk. Time I put you in your place!" Carly yelled.

Ile laughed at the thought. "Well, child, let's see about that, shall we?"

Noah, Simon, and Hunter stopped and looked at one another with fear of what was to come. The crew of both boats hit the deck.

Carly's eyes lit up as green as could be, and the wizard's eyes did the same—but red. Carly waved her hand, and a bolt of lightning flew out, hitting one of the masts on the pirate ship. They heard the sound of cracking wood as it began to fall. The crew ran for cover, and the wizard went to do the same, but Carly unleashed her powers on him. The powers met between the two—Carly pushing her bright green light of energy toward the wizard as he pushed back. The wizard grew angrier. He was having a hard time stopping Carly. Just then, he waved his staff with more power, knocking Carly to the deck. Everything stopped for a moment.

The pirate boat was a mess, and Captain Black ordered the crew to throw the hooks to catch the *Drifter*. Through the air the hooks came and wrapped around the mast of the *Drifter*. Black's crew tied the lines tightly down so they could not get away once again.

Now with Carly standing back up with her staff giving the wizard an evil stare, the crew of both boats knew it was time to duck, all hell would break out any second now. Cappy began to wake up after that hit from the wizard, slowly turning to see Carly—his daughter—and the wizard get ready to stand off. Just before he could speak, they let loose on one another once again.

The *Drifter* had been caught. Carly was in no mood, and that wizard was going to have more than he bargained for. They were tearing both boats up with the power they both held within. With all their anger, Carly and the wizard became weaker as time went on. Noah didn't know how much more both ships could take. Just then, a woman came out, and in one burst, Carly was knocked to the deck, powerless.

It was Sarah. She turned and looked at Ile and said, "Enough!" Ile just looked at her, waiting for her to turn on him, as well.

Cappy looked at Sarah. They both had tears in their eyes. Ile was beaten down by Carly. Sarah had stopped this fight before her daughter was hurt. She knew this was her daughter.

There would be no other with such power, and being with Cappy, well, that was enough. Everything stopped just like that. *Drifter* was caught, and so was the crew. Both boats were now tided side by side, *Drifter* with her mast damaged and broken planks alongside from crashing into the ship. All that work, and in less than twenty minutes, the boat was a wreck.

Captain Black's ship had taken a beating, as well—one mast lying over from Carly hitting it with her powers in a rage. Their sails had lots of holes from the burning coal fired at them from the *Drifter*. They came aboard with swords and took the crew off the *Drifter* and onto the *Dark Spirit*. Noah and Hunter were brought on first, seeing all the damage they had done to Black's ship. Then Carly, Simon, and Cappy were pulled up, as well. They all stood along the rail of the mighty pirate ship as Captain Black paced in front of them silently.

The *Dark Spirit* was over a hundred years old, and you could see they had put it back together before from battle. Splintered wood was everywhere, but it still looked like a solid ship.

Black looked at Noah and said, "My boy, you gave a good fight for such a young man."

Noah didn't say a word.

Black looked at Cappy. "Well, old friend," he said.

Cappy quickly spoke out. "You were never a friend of mine!" Cappy demanded to see Sarah.

Black laughed. "In time, old man."

Black's crew was busy pulling the mast back up and getting

out spare sails. It looked like they were getting ready to leave in the very near future. You could tell they had done this many times. The carpenters were out fixing the damaged wood, and sailmakers worked on the spare sails to replace them quickly. Black ordered his mate to take the *Drifter's* crew to the brig—the jail on the boat. As they went down in the large ship, it had a very damp smell, and the wood looked much older inside. They went down two decks to reach the brig. The jail keeper opened the rusty, old door for them to go inside their new home for the time being. As he closed the rusty door, it gave off a screeching noise that raised the hair on the backs of their necks. Then the door banged shut and they heard the click of the lock. There they stayed, under guard by a man who sat behind a short wall so he could see them. As soon as the mate walked away, the jail keeper lay down on his bench to take a nap. They had not seen Sarah. Cappy sat down along with the rest of the *Drifter's* crew.

Noah said softly, "We need to find a way out."

Cappy looked at him for a moment and said, "I want you all to rest for now. I'm sure Black and Ile will be back for a talk later."

The Escape

Time passed as the crew of the *Drifter* slept after all that had happened. The rusty door opening again woke them all. There was Black and his mate, smiling, and another man carried food in for them. The hungry crew dug into what looked like food.

Simon choked as he forced his dinner down.

Black looked at Cappy and said, "Did you really think you could take this ship?" Cappy stared down as Black laughed. "I take it this is Carly, Sarah's daughter." Black looked at Carly. "It's very nice to meet you. Wish it were under better terms. I have promised Sarah if she stays aboard without any trouble, I will not hurt any of you, as we had already in the past made this deal."

Cappy snapped out, "What is it you want from her? You have the wizard."

Black laughed. "Better to have two so-called wizards, don't you think? Enjoy your meal. We set sail in the morning."

Cappy yelled out, "To where?"

Black turned around with a straight face and said, "Into the past, old friend. I have three wizards now. Nothing can stop us from taking the treasures of the past into the present, and they are worth so much more." He turned and walked away.

On the way down to the jail, Noah had seen where the gunpowder for the cannons was kept, and so did Cappy. They all came together in a circle to talk. Cappy knew how the ship was built. After all, he was a shipbuilder. They would need a distraction. Somehow, they needed to turn the ship's wheel all the way over and take the chains hanging on the wall to lock the rudder in place. This way, they would not be able to steer and just go in circles. Cappy told Noah he would ask to speak with Black alone up where they steered the ship. Carly would wait until the jail keeper fell asleep once again to get his keys with her powers of moving things. Hunter would bring Simon to the back of the ship where the steering was. They needed to stop the rudder from moving. Noah had to find a way to turn the wheel over to one side while talking to Black from the ship's helm. Hunter would have to go with Simon to do this. He worked on boats, as well, and Simon was smaller and could get in the corner to fasten that rudder. When they were done, the boat would only go in circles, giving them time to get away. Now with this plan in place, they would have to wait to see how many of Black's crew moved around the ship. This way, they would know when the crew changed shifts by watching them and observing how often they came through the boat. That would tell them the best time to make their move. It could take a few days to learn how Black ran his ship, but they only had this one day, so they hoped their plan would still work.

The wizard had a pocketful of scrolls. Carly needed to get them so they couldn't jump though time. With just a handful of words from the wizard, they could travel though time and go anywhere. It wouldn't be easy to get that close to the wizard without him knowing. Carly had her book and staff along with her scrolls on the *Drifter*. Ile did not know this. How would they pull this off? Only time would tell.

They began to watch how the crew worked aboard ship. This would tell them in time when to make their move safely and how much time they had to do it. Well, the crew of the *Drifter* watched as the *Dark Spirit's* crew changed the guard watching them every three hours, and a crew member did a walk through the boat every two hours, checking to make sure that there were no problems. They had four hours until both the jail keeper and the watchmen changed at the same time. So as the time neared, Noah asked to talk to the captain right before they changed shifts. He was granted his request and was brought right where he wanted to be—at the ship's wheel up top.

Black said, "Young man, you are very brave taking on this ship with such a small, limited vessel."

Noah was leaning on the wheel. Since the boat was sitting dead in the water for repairs, there would be no one at the helm. So Noah turned the wheel every time the captain looked away.

Noah asked, "Why do you want Sarah so badly?"

Black looked at him without words. He looked angry. Then

turned to tell him why, while the captain had his back turned Noah spun the wheel hard over then just leaned on it.

Black said, "That's the only way the wizard will stay aboard. Without him, we can't jump through time." Then he looked Noah right in the eyes. "Did you know I was born over a hundred years ago?"

Noah just looked at him. Black looked all of forty at the most. "How can that be?" Noah asked.

Black just looked at the young man before speaking. "Jumping though time has slowed down time for everyone on this vessel. How do you think Ile looks the same after so many years? I will do what he asks to keep him here. That means Sarah must stay. Now, my boy, we must decide what to do with you and your brave crew."

Shortly after Noah went up to see the captain, Carly used her powers to lift the keys from the sleeping guard to open the locked jail door. Opening the door very slowly to let Hunter and Simon out, Cappy went back to where they held the gunpowder and fuses to set it off. There, he would put a long fuse leading to a barrel, blowing up what he hoped to be the only gunpowder they had for the cannons. Then, he would make his way to the cannon that stuck out the door on the side of the boat. Then, he would climb down onto the *Drifter*, ready to start her engine and escape. While down there, he would place a knife near every rope holding the *Drifter* to the pirate ship for the crew to cut her loose.

Now with Simon and Hunter climbing through the compartments full of rats and water, still making their way back to the rudder. Hunter was carrying the chains to stop the steering from working on Black's ship. Carly stayed behind to stop anyone from catching them. She was told to go easy on anyone that tried.

Simon and Hunter finally could see the rudder, but Simon had to go the rest of the way himself, because Hunter just couldn't fit. Hunter passed the chains to Simon, and Simon pulled them over to a steel pole and then wrapped the rudder with chain. After that, he pulled it tight, wrapping it to the steel pole so the rudder wouldn't move. The ship had no steering, but Black would not find this out until later. Then, Simon wrapped it around everything he could find, making it hard to get off for the crew of this ship when they realized the ship only was able to do circles. Simon crawled back out, and they started their way back.

Cappy had already set up the bomb, and it had a long fuse. Cappy was climbing out the door of the cannon when he heard Black walking his way to look over the rail of the ship.

He stopped when Noah yelled, "Look! Is that a ship?"

Black ran to the other side, allowing Cappy to get on the *Drifter*. Simon and Hunter were back, and Hunter tapped on the guard's head. The man's eye's sprung wide open. Hunter quickly grabbed his arms while Simon gagged him with a dirty sock so none of the crew could hear. Hunter held the large man while Carly and Simon tied up the smelly pirate. After a lengthy struggle, the guard found himself in the jail cell. Quickly, they ran for the doorway and then waited for the big bang. They waited and waited. Cappy thought that maybe the fuse had gone out. Noah was already out and up on deck with

Black when, all of a sudden, the boat shuddered with a bang ... then another and another.

"Wow!" Hunter yelled. "I thought he was only doing one barrel of powder."

Carly had disappeared. She ran down to meet her mother. The boys went after her. Before she could reach the corner, Ile stepped in Carly's path. Carly stepped back and began to get ready to let him have it. Simon and Hunter backed up. This was going to be ugly. But just as the wizard went to wave his hand, Sarah came around the corner and let him have it until he went to his knees and passed out. Little did the wizard know, she was much more powerful than he'd thought. Carly ran to her mother, hugging her.

They both began to cry. Simon said, "We really have to go."

Sarah looked down at Carly with tears in her eyes and heard her mother's voice for the first time. "Look at you, so big and beautiful. Take this letter, my child."

Sarah bent over, taking the scrolls from the wizard's pocket as he was just starting to wake.

"Read this letter when you're safe. I'm sorry, I must stay."

Crying, Carly asked, "Why?"

"You must go now, quickly," Sarah insisted. "I will always hold you in my heart!"

Hunter struggled to pull Carly down the hall and get her off the ship. Carly looked back the whole time as the wizard began to stand. They had just turned the corner when they heard Sarah and the wizard fighting with large blasts of light glowing throughout the ship as the two battled. Then, it stopped. They were out on deck, and Black's men were running all over the place, putting fires out. Noah was still up at the helm with Black as he shouted at the men. Carly, Simon, and Hunter were jumping onto the *Drifter* in the middle of this mess. Just as they stood up from the jump, Noah swung on a rope right over the top of the *Drifter* and let go—right into the water. He missed the boat. Hunter ran to the side and pulled him back onto the *Drifter*. Just then, there was another big bang. The wires that held the mast up on the *Dark Spirit* parted, and down came the mast once again. With the engine running, they cut the lines holding the *Drifter* to the ship and made a run for it. The wizard came walking out on deck, watching them pulling away from the ship. He looked really bad after the fight with Sarah, but was Sarah okay? Carly, with tears in her eyes, waved her hands up. The look in her eyes was empty. The wizard looked scared for the first time. He ducked. Carly let loose such a blast of energy that the ship began to lay on its side. Everything was lifting off the deck and flying through the air. She pushed harder. The ship was on the verge of rolling over. The crew of the *Dark Spirit* held onto the rails for dear life.

Cappy yelled, "Carly! Carly, that's enough!"

Carly slowly dropped her hands and fell to the deck. Cappy ran over to her. She was barely breathing after that. The pirate ship was in shambles, still lying over but not as bad. All the cargo had moved on Black's ship to one side when she laid the ship over. The crew rushed to get the cargo back to the other side to stop the boat from lying over. She was taking on water and would sink if they did not move quickly. The *Drifter* with heavy damage as well when the engine stopped, they were dead in the water. Both boats were disabled about a few hundred feet from one another. Noah and Cappy looked at Black and Ile. Both were looking back at them with anger in their eyes.

Both crews had problems, and their fight would have to wait. Cappy kneeled on the side of Carly and put a damp cloth on her head. She was in rough shape. They needed to get a sail up quickly. The wizard didn't need a scroll to jump in time. He knew all of the scrolls by heart. Hunter and Simon went to work on the sails and the broken wires that held the mast up. Noah worked on the engine as Cappy took care of Carly. Cappy looked down. There was a letter hanging out of Carly's pocket along with some scrolls. He pulled it out. It was from Sarah, but he would not read it without asking. Cappy put the scrolls and her letter down below deck to keep them safe, and when he did so, he saw that she had brought the book and her own scrolls.

Now, the two ships lay beside one another, both not able to sail away. Cappy started working on the sails to get at least one really good one. But at the same time, there was no wind for either boat to go anywhere. Both crews worked hard to fix their boats. *Drifter* needed to get out of there—they knew this. But Black had a mess on his ship keeping them busy. Carly had ripped that thing apart.

Carly was starting to come around, and she sat up once again. Cappy ran over to her. "You must rest," he said.

Carly looked to the side of them, and there was the *Dark Spirit*.

"Why did you stop me?" she asked Cappy.

"Carly," he said, "we didn't come to hurt anyone. This is something we will never do. We help others. That's how your mother was, and I am the same."

Carly's eyes began to tear once again. She said, "Cappy, I think the wizard hurt my mother."

Cappy looked down for a moment and then said, "I don't think that happened. Your mother is much more powerful than you think."

At the same time, Cappy prayed his words were true. Simon came over to Carly and asked if she could jump the *Drifter* through time before the *Dark Spirit* came for them. Carly reached for her scrolls, but they were gone along with her mother's letter.

Cappy said with a smile, "They are under your pillow down below."

Carly was relieved to hear that he'd put them in a safe place. She ran down and came back with a handful of scrolls. She was still learning the book, never mind the scrolls. She looked up at Cappy and said, "I can do this, but I don't know where we will end up."

Noah yelled, "We have no choice! Just do it!"

The wizard and Captain Black were watching. Ile knew.

He could see his scrolls. He yelled, "Go wherever you like. I will find you!"

Just then, Sarah walked down toward the wizard. She looked hurt but alive. Cappy waved. He'd never had a chance to hold her once again.

Carly yelled, "Mother, I can't leave you!"

The wizard smiled.

"You must, child. We will see each other again, I promise," said Sarah.

Carly spoke the words of one scroll, and the wind began to circle the vessel. White light was so bright that one couldn't see. Their bodies felt like they were floating around in the air, and—poof!—they were gone. The wizard heard the words she spoke and wouldn't be far behind.

The Big Jump in Time

They were flying through time for the first time. Simon was screaming at the top of his lungs. Everyone else was hanging on for dear life. The boat was just floating in the air, spinning like a ride at the carnival. All of a sudden, they felt a big bump as water splashed up into the sky. Slowly, the bright light went away, and the sun was shining all around them. They were on the side of an island filled with trees, and there was no sign of a house anywhere. The beach had bright, white sand but very few rocks on the beach itself. There were more islands all in one big row. There had to have been at least five others just as beautiful. There were what looked to be passages between each island. But you could see the rocks sticking out of the water over there, not a place to bring a boat through. Deer swam across from one island to the other. What a place this was—as if time really had stopped there.

The *Drifter* was badly damaged. The wooden planks were splintered and broken all down the side of the vessel. The mast tip was gone. Wires that held it strongly in place from the force of wind that pushes on the sails were broke as well. But the mast still stood. Cappy had brought hand tools for fixing the boat. He knew this would happen. It looked like there was plenty of wood on that island. Now, they had to go get what was needed to fix the old girl up and sail once again.

There was something about that island, said Cappy—like he had seen it before.

Carly had to get reading to know how they would get back home. Before they could even start for the beach, there was a big ship quickly heading their way.

Simon sat down and said, "Not again. Can you believe this?"

Noah asked Cappy, "How could they find us so quickly?"

Looking in the distance, Cappy said, "Kids, I don't think that's Captain Black's ship."

"What do you mean you don't think that that is him?" said Noah.

"Well, Noah, that ship looks like a British warship." Cappy just stared.

Simon held his hand on his head and said, "Just what we need."

Hunter stood ready by the cannons. Cappy saw the ship's cannon doors open. Then, out came their cannons.

"Hunter," he said, "don't do that. We're in no shape for another fight."

Why did this vessel have no flag? It must be yet another pirate ship. Now, Simon was breathing into a bag. He'd had enough for one day. The ship was really moving and full sail on. Just before they looked like they were going to be rammed and looking up at this fierce vessel. The ship turned hard, dropping the anchors. Slowly, the ship came to a stop with all her cannons pointing right at the *Drifter*. All the sails came down at once. There was silence. Hunter, Carly, and the whole crew just looked. Carly had that look in her eyes, and Cappy had to settle her down. The two ships just sat side by side. The crew of the *Drifter* looked up at the large ship. This vessel looked very new.

Cappy said, "Crew, I think we went back in time over a hundred years."

The flag went up—it was British. But why hadn't the crew come over to look? Moments later, the whole crew of the ship was staring down at the *Drifter*. They were young kids with a very large ship. None of them spoke a word. Just then, a young man wearing a black leather hat walked through the crowd looking down upon the beaten vessel. He took off his hat and tipped his head.

The man said, "My name is Captain Bell. How may we assist you?"

The crew of the *Drifter* let out an exhale.

"Thank God!" said Simon as the man smiled upon the crew.

Cappy said, "We had a battle with a ship called—"

Bell said, "Let me guess. You had a run in with *Dark Spirit* and Captain Black's renegade crew, not to mention that wizard of his."

Cappy looked shocked. Bell looked at him and said, "We've been chasing Black for years. My father before me went to find him and was never seen again. I vowed to catch this pirate when I was a child. They have stolen much from our queen, not to mention ships that don't return."

Bell told Cappy that he'd made a vow to catch this pirate in the name of his father. "The queen has given me and the crew this ship to hunt the *Dark Spirit*. Black has taken someone from all who ride this vessel. We will hunt the *Dark Spirit* until the end of time."

"What is your ship's name?" asked Cappy.

Bell smiled and replied, "*Huntress!*"

Noah giggled. "Now, that's a fitting name!"

Captain Bell and the *Huntress*

Captain Bell had grown up on the ocean like his father. His father was a captain on one of the queen's many ships. After many years at sea, the ship did not return. The queen's ships had been having trouble with the *Dark Spirit* and Captain Black, that is. They just could not catch him. Now, when Bell became older, he would join the queen's Navy and in time he would have a chance at a ship of his own. Time had passed for Bell. He wanted that ship to hunt the *Dark Spirit*. He asked to see the queen one day while in port. He had made it up the ladder to being a mate for a few years. He asked to hunt this pirate. The queen knew something would have to be done about this problem with Black. They had a large ship that was taken out of her fleet because it needed lots of repairs to be seaworthy once again.

She told Bell, "I will grant you the *Huntress*. You are to get your own crew. I will let you fly our flag, and you will have to do this on your own." The queen looked at Bell—the tall, skinny young man with very long hair—once again. "I will have my carpenters fix the ship to be ready for sea. You gather a crew, and we will stock the ship with what you need. After that, young man, you're on your own. I know your father was one of my captains. We had spoken many times. He was a great man. I wish you a safe journey."

A man came around and handed a flag to Bell. That's how he made captain and received his ship. The queen thought highly of his father. She hoped he would bring Black to her to answer for what he had done.

Bell told this story to the crew of the *Drifter* in detail this time. He invited them aboard the *Huntress* for dinner. Needless to say, that was the talk around the table. The *Drifter* lay tied to the *Huntress* for that night. In the morning, he let Noah take one of his small boats to the beach to gather wood with some of his crew. Hunter stayed behind with Cappy, working on the *Drifter*.

Bell looked down the next morning with a big smile. "How are we doing down there?" he asked with a smile from ear to ear.

Hunter thought he smiled too much, but Cappy thought the man was true to his words. Carly went ashore with Simon and Noah, along with some of Bell's crew. They cut ten trees down to bring back. The *Drifter* needed some new planks and maybe a whole side of the boat replaced. The boat had been through hell and back with that wizard and Black. Bell had sent his crew with a second boat, so they had enough help to get the wood back. Six hours later, the small boats had their trees in tow behind them, heading for the *Huntress*. They would use the *Huntress* to cut the wood and fit new planks. Where she was a very big ship this made things much easier to work on. They came alongside the *Huntress*, one boat at a time. The crew grabbed the lines tied to the trees. One at a time, they pulled aboard tree after tree until they were all on the deck of the *Huntress*. Cappy and Bell's carpenters cut the planks for the side of the boat from the trees they had brought to the ship.

Now, Bell knew that, in a moment's notice, another ship could come looking for a fight. So Bell had his crew help fix the small boat to get them under way once again. Faster would be better with Black lingering around somewhere.

The whole crew cut the wood to the size Cappy and Hunter needed. Simon and Noah fastened the planks back in place one at a time. This went on for a few days. Carly had seen a young man hovering in the air sleeping—just floating there.

Bell walked up on the side of Carly and laughed. "That would be Dizzy."

"Dizzy! You mean he's dizzy?" Carly look a bit confused.

"Well, no, that's his name," Bell laughed. "You don't think we survived this long without a wizard of our own, do you?"

Dizzy lifted his ragged hat to take a look at this girl who was so interested in who he was.

Carly asked, "Where are you from?"

Dizzy laughed. "Who knows."

This made Carly angry, and Dizzy pulled his hat back down to sleep. Carly sent him over the side of the boat and into the water. The crew came running. Cappy quickly climbed back on the *Huntress*. He thought Bell would be angry about this. But Bell looked over the side, laughing along with the whole crew of the *Huntress*.

"Dizzy, you really did need a bath, you know," Bell said,

turning and looking at Carly. "Now I know why Black didn't take your ship."

They all began to laugh, not Dizzy as he floated through the air back on the boat to see Carly.

"So what would your name be?" asked Dizzy, looking at Carly as he wrung out his hat.

"Carly. My name is Carly, and you don't seem very nice to me."

Dizzy laughed. "Well, I just like to keep to myself until they need me."

"From the looks of it, you could be more help," said Carly.

Dizzy smiled. "But I am."

Carly was frustrated with him, but they had something in common.

Dizzy looked at Carly with a straight face. "I really don't know where I from. That was not a lie."

Carly felt bad and said she was sorry for throwing him overboard, with a smile.

Night came, and the crew was close to finishing all the repairs with so much help. Bell offered them dry bunks to sleep in on the *Huntress*. They would finish up in the morning and part ways. Noah and his crew didn't refuse that offer. Simon was sleeping in his clothes again ten minutes later. He didn't waste any time. The crew was sleeping, but Bell had guards on the deck, looking out for other ships—namely, the *Dark Spirit*. Carly was up on deck staring into the moonlight. Cappy came up and put his hand on her head. Don't worry, things will be fine. Cappy went back down to get some rest, but Carly spent the night out on deck, wondering about her mother. Soon, she fell asleep on the deck of the ship.

The next morning, Dizzy went over and woke Carly. He hadn't slept well.

"Carly, I need to talk to you," said Dizzy.

Carly tried to open her eyes. "What is it, Dizzy?"

"I can't help but think that you have powers like me."

Looking up at Dizzy, Carly said, "You woke me up for that?"

"Yes!" said Dizzy. "I hide it well, but I have felt alone my whole life until now."

Carly stood up, feeling bad for giving Dizzy a hard time after waking her. Now, they both sat and talked about how they felt. Carly decided to show Dizzy all the scrolls and the book her mother had left. Carly told Dizzy of her mother being on Black's ship. Dizzy's eyes were wide as could be.

"Carly," he said, "I must tell you something."

Carly was all ears to hear what it was Dizzy had to say.

"Your mother has saved our lives more than once," Dizzy told his new friend.

"What do you mean?" asked Carly.

"Well, as we battled the wizard we began to lose, more than once. Each time the wizard was about to finish the *Huntress* off, the woman would appear and strike him down with her powers, giving us time to get away. Your mother is the reason we are still here trying to fight this ship. Bell feels we will sooner or later get the best of the *Dark Spirit* with or without your mother's help. Then this can be over. Bell has made it very clear that the crew is to not fire the cannons anywhere she would be and to protect her at all cost. Bell felt he owed this to the woman that saved his ship and crew."

Carly thought, *Maybe that's why she will not leave.*

Dizzy looked at Carly and said, "I know she has saved many ships."

Things started to make sense. Carly told Dizzy she needed to speak with Cappy, who was down on the boat doing repairs with the crew. Carly ran over and climbed down the side of the *Huntress*, jumped on the *Drifter*, and pulled Cappy aside. She told him all that Dizzy had said to her. Cappy smiled and then started to laugh. Carly, looking angry, asked what was so funny about that.

"Carly, your mother wanted to save the world every day. This was something she could do to make things better. That's why she will not leave the ship. But if we could get control of the ship and stop them, she could," said Cappy.

Bell was on the *Drifter* with three members of his crew, finishing the last things to be done. But Bell had never seen some of the things they had on the boat, which was very different from his own. They were done.

Bell yelled to Cappy and Noah, "You mind if we take her out for a quick sail, Would be a nice change."

Noah looked at Cappy. He turned at Bell and said, "Go for it. Have some fun."

Bell grabbed a few crew members that wanted to take a ride on this ship from the future, none of them had ever seen such a vessel. They all jumped on, and the crew of the *Huntress* threw the lines off, setting them free. Off went Bell, smiling as he did. They were sailing all over the place, having a ball. They went so far Noah could barely see them. Then they turned and started heading back. It was nice to see the *Drifter* from here and see how she looked underway sailing—that was something none of them had seen. Just then, the sky became dark, and the wind became stronger by the second. Captain Black was coming, and the *Drifter* was too far away. There was a bright flash. Everyone had to turn away from the brightness filling the sky. Their eyes could not take such light. There it was, *Dark Spirit*, side by side with Bell on the *Drifter*. The crew of the *Huntress* began to panic. They could not help their captain and crew.

They turned to Noah and said, "Captain, you must take command of the ship. We have two wizards with powers. Maybe now we can stop Black."

Looking at Dizzy, Carly said, "Let's do it. Time for Ile to get what's coming to him."

Carly had just brought all the scrolls and the book aboard

to show *Dizzy*, not forgetting her staff, thank God. You could see the fireballs being launched at Black from the *Drifter*. Fire flying everywhere, Noah ordered the crew to haul the anchor fast. But just as the anchor broke the water, they could see the fireballs had stopped. Black once again had the *Drifter*. Noah yelled to Hunter and Bell's crew to send up the sails. With their anchor up and one sail raised, they began to move toward the *Dark Spirit*. The second sail went up, in moments filling with wind, they were gaining speed. They were now close enough to fire cannons.

Bell's crew asked, "Do you want the forward cannons ready to fire?"

"Yes!" yelled Noah.

Noah looked at Cappy and said, "Fire at will, but don't hit the *Drifter*."

One at a time, the cannons went off, sounding like thunder. The whole boat shuddered. Now Black being fired upon, he sent a few back at the *Huntress*. One cannonball fell right in front of the boat. But the next went right through the bow. Wood flew everywhere, leaving a big hole it the front of the ship. Nonetheless, they kept going for the *Dark Spirit*.

Noah yelled, "Fire! Fire!"

Two misses but one right through the back of Black's ship. Now gaining on Black who had the *Drifter* alongside slowing him down, they could see Bell and the crew fighting them off from boarding the *Drifter*. Then, yet another thundering blast filled the air, coming from the bow cannons on the *Huntress*.

You could hear the cracking of wood in the distance. Slowly, the new mast on the *Drifter* came crashing down. The boat was once again in shambles. They were taking Bell and his men on board.

Noah still yelled at the crew, "Fire the cannons!"

Once again, Black fired first, thunder and yet another hit on the *Huntress*, the crew ducking and wood flying through the air once again. Then, the *Huntress* fired both bow cannons at once, the crew holding their ears from the lingering echo throughout the ship. It felt as if the boat came to a stop when they fired the cannons. The crew watched closely as both shots hit the stern of Black's ship. Black's crew was running out of the way. Pieces of wood went flying into the water. Now, you could see right in the *Dark Spirit*. Carly and Dizzy both stood under the sails, lifting their arms then turned their hands up, the sail began to bulge with more wind. The *Huntress* was really moving now, and both ships were ready to fire once again. One big flash and the wind sent the sails in the opposite direction pushing the crew to the deck with force on the *Huntress*. They had finally done it, they jumped. The *Drifter* went with them as well. Bell and his crew were gone, just like that. There was silence on the ship; not a word said. Cappy looked at Noah as you could hear a pin drop with the silence. Noah gave the order to drop one of the sails as he turned back toward the island. The whole crew was speechless—not a word was spoken about what had happened before their eyes. As they came closer, the other sail came down, as well.

Noah shouted out, "Drop the anchor! We will be here for a while!"

Noah Takes Command of the *Huntress*

The anchor grabbed, and the ship came to a stop. There was silence as the crew stared off into the distance where Bell and the *Drifter* were last seen. The crew began loudly arguing over what to do now that Bell was gone. Cappy stood up from the helm, looking down on the crew. *What a mess,* he thought. Noah was silent. Carly and Dizzy stood up on the bow of the boat, looking down on all the damage they had taken from Black's cannons. Simon looked mighty grim sitting on the deck, but Hunter went over to give him a pat on the back, telling Simon that things would be okay.

Cappy gave a yell, but the crew didn't hear him. Cappy became upset. Once gain, he yelled. Finally, they stopped arguing. There the crew stood, looking up at Cappy standing by Noah at the ship's helm.

Cappy stared at them hard. "This will stop now!" He looked at Noah and said, "The ship is yours for the time being. Give the order."

Noah looked at Cappy and then turned his head toward the crew. "We will chase him down, I promise you this. But we need to fix the *Huntress* first. Now, lower the lifeboats and head for the island once again."

Noah told them to cut as much wood as they could fit in the cargo hold. This was where they would store enough wood for a few battles, the way things were going. The crew stood there.

Noah yelled once again, "Did you not hear me? I am the captain for the time being. Now get to it!"

Grabbing gather their tools, the crew scattered and lowered the boats.

Noah called Hunter to the helm. "Hunter," he said, "I want you to go with them."

Hunter just looked at Noah. "Why?" he asked. "I would be more help here."

"I know," said Noah, "and you will. But I want the crew from both ships working together. Bring back a good piece of wood for a new mast for the *Drifter*."

"But why?" asked Hunter.

"Because I will get her back, and from the looks of that last battle, it needs one."

Hunter headed for one of the lifeboats, knowing he would be of much more help on the *Huntress*. Hunter understood what Noah was doing—uniting the two crews was in the best interest of the ship and trust between them. Carly and Dizzy still stood on the bow.

"Carly," Noah yelled, "you and Dizzy get back here. We need to talk. Simon, you too. I have a job for all of you."

Cappy gathered the carpenters and headed to the bow of the *Huntress* to start replacing all the broken wood—not to mention the two big holes in the ship. The tools came out, and Cappy and the crew started fixing the beaten-down vessel. The small boats went to shore, gathering wood for repairs. The crew planned to bring more than needed, never can have enough wood with cannonballs flying around. Now, with Noah's crew up near the ship's wheel, they had their talk. Noah told Carly and Dizzy to get studying the book and scrolls so they could jump with the hope of landing where Black could be. Simon was to study the charts on the ship. They were much different, being made over a hundred years ago. The charts lacked detail and information back then. With all of this going on, Noah would go to Bell's cabin, reading the ship's logs to see Bell's notes on what had happened in the past. Noah hoped this could help them now. He needed to know everything he could about Black and his ship. Since they were going to pick another fight, this time would be different—Noah had the *Huntress*. The day went by, and the small boats made many trips to the island, bringing back wood and whatever supplies they could find. Now, the whole crew was working on fixing the ship. But after a very long day, Noah called to them to gather once again. As they stood there, looking tired as could be, Noah asked them to sit down for a moment. The crew sat on the deck, looking up at Noah.

After a moment, Noah said, "You all did a fine job and are by far the best crew a captain could have. Now, I want you all to get some rest. We have a lot of repairs before we're going anywhere."

The smell of dinner was in the air. The weary crew went for a quick bite and then straight to their bunks for some rest. Noah kept two guards up to walk the deck and keep a lookout. They would switch off so they had some rest come daybreak. Keeping a lookout at all times was a must. The wizard did say he would find them. Noah wasn't up for any surprises. The sun set, and all would sleep for now, anyway.

Morning came fast, and the crew woke. The cook had made fresh bacon, and the smell of homemade bread lingered in the air. That was enough to wake everyone but Simon. He would sleep though anything like any other day. Hunter went to wake Simon so he didn't miss out on breakfast. After a short but great meal, the crew went to work putting the ship back together once again. Some were tightening up the rigging wires holding the mast up, and the rest were cutting and fitting new planks for the bow. It took many planks to fill in the big holes Black's ship put in the *Huntress*. You could walk right through them—that's how big they were.

The day went on with the sound of saws and hammers working away. Carly and Dizzy had found a way to jump—but to where, they didn't know. They ran up to tell Noah, who was working with Simon reading charts.

"Noah," yelled Carly, "we can jump!"

Noah smiled. "I knew you two would figure that out."

"Well," said Dizzy, "we can jump, but I don't know where we will land." He laughed.

Scratching his head, Noah said, "Well, that's a start. Keep working on it. We will be doing the same here."

Another few days went by, and the ship was back to normal. Once again, Noah gathered the crew for a speech.

"We will set sail in the morning," he told the crew. Carly and Dizzy thought it would be a good idea to jump right where Black did. They had Ile's scrolls—there were four of them. That didn't mean there weren't more, but they were the few he had in his pocket. Now, one of the scrolls looked very worn out. Noah thought that could be the one. Noah asked Carly to use the worn scroll when they jumped. They all could see that one scroll had been used many times. The day had once again come to an end. The crew went to their bunks for some much-needed rest. Noah did the same. Cappy stayed up for a while, talking to Carly. He told her not to worry and that they would find her mother again. Hunter and Simon both went up on the bow to sleep. They thought the fresh air would do them some good.

Carly looked at Cappy and began to cry. "I haven't read her letter yet. I'm just not ready."

Cappy held her. "That's fine, child. You will when you're ready."

They both went down to take a nap. Tomorrow would come fast.

The Hunt for Captain Bell

Morning came, and the crew woke, not to the smell of breakfast cooking, but to the sound of thundering cannons in the near distance. Noah's crew all ran to the deck, thinking Black was back and attacking the *Huntress*. Noah sprung out of bed, dressing as he ran for the helm. Cappy was right behind him as they climbed the stairs. Noah quickly grabbed his spyglass and began to focus on the ships.

Cappy heard Noah exhale, and he asked, "What is it, Noah?'

"Well, it's not Captain Black," Noah said.

In the distance, there were two ships battling it out. Smoke filled the air as the cannons fired. The sound of cracking wood echoed through the air.

Noah yelled down to the crew, "Haul anchor, and get a sail up!"

Noah didn't know if they would come for them. Carly was controlling her powers lately, but she and Dizzy ran to the helm to speak with Noah. Cappy was making his way to the sails with the crew and Hunter. Simon was still sleeping.

One of the ships looked like it was in trouble. Noah held the spyglass up to get a better look. The ship in trouble was one of the queen's ships. They were taking a beating from the pirates. Things didn't look good. The anchor broke the water, and they were under way to help this doomed ship. It was the queen's ship, after all.

Noah yelled to the crew, "Ready the cannons!"

"What side?" Hunter yelled.

"Both!" Noah shouted.

Hunter was helping push the cannons in place, wondering why Noah would want both sides of the ship ready to fire.

That's when Carly came to Noah. "After this, we will jump, right?"

"Yes, Carly. Let's help the queen's ship first."

Dizzy looked at Carly and said, "Don't worry—there are two of us now."

They were gaining speed but not fast enough.

Noah yelled, "Carly, now would be a good time!"

She turned with a smile. "Finally!"

Dizzy looked at Carly. "Finally, what?" he asked with a grin.

Carly, on one knee, raised her hands. Her eyes lit up once

again. Dizzy smiled. He had never seen anyone like himself other than the wizard. Carly pushed her hands forward, and the sail filled with more wind, tighter and tighter, until the wood creaked from under the mast.

Noah yelled down, "Not too hard, Carly!"

Huntress was moving now. Dizzy was smiling and ready for a fight, as well. All the cannons were manned, and Cappy was on the bow keeping watch. They were almost there.

Hunter yelled, "What side are we firing from once again?"

Noah looked at the two ships. "Both!"

"Both!" The crew repeated after Noah with fear in their eyes.

"Yes, we're going right between them." Noah had a funny look in his eyes.

They all looked at Noah like he was crazy.

"Did you say 'both'?"

"Yes, both!" Noah yelled once again.

The *Huntress* was moving full bore. Noah spun the wheel side to side, trying to keep the *Huntress* on course, still heading right between the ships and their cannons. The *Huntress* was all over the place. Noah had a hard time steering. Breathing heavily, Noah spun the wheel until the bow was finally going in one direction. Noah was barely able to talk as the sweat poured down his face. He leaned on the wheel. *Huntress* was finally making her way right in and was nearly halfway in between the other vessels.

At the last minute, he yelled, "Ready both anchors!"

"Both!" they yelled.

"Yes, one on each side at the same time!"

Noah grew frustrated with having to repeat himself. "We will drop them both to slow the boat down."

"Cappy," Noah yelled, "when the anchors drop, drop the sails too!"

Cappy looked at Noah with a grin, thinking this is one brave man, or crazy.

Carly stopped pushing on the sails and then walked over by Dizzy.

Dizzy looked at Carly. "Nice trick."

Carly grinned and said, "Show me what you've got."

"I will," said Dizzy.

Just as the *Huntress* was about to pass between the ships, Noah yelled, "Drop the anchors!" Down they went—and fast.

The *Huntress* slowly slid right between the two mighty vessels, still trying to stop.

Noah yelled at Simon now, "Raise the flag so they don't fire on us, Simon!"

Simon was barely awake, pulling the flag up as fast as he could. Noah watched the captain on the queen's ship, hoping he wouldn't fire on them. Noah still watched and was ready to fire on both ships if needed. The queen's captain was pointing at the flag.

The ship began to slow to a stop. "Fire!" yelled Noah.

The *Huntress* laid to the side as all twenty cannons fired at once, cannonballs passing each other from the two ships, as the fight began protecting the queen's ship. The pirates were running for cover. Then, the sound of smashing wood echoed through the air. They were reloading for another shot. The British ship took a hit. Her mast was falling over into the water. One of the cannonballs from the pirate ship took it down. Carly's eyes filled with green fire, her hand ready to unleash hell on the renegade ship. Carly caught a glimpse of Dizzy out of the corner of her eye. There was Dizzy with his eyes bright as could be and green, as well.

Dizzy looked at Carly. "Shall we?" he said as his smile faded away.

Dizzy's eyes turned a fiery green. Carly turned with her eyes full of rage to stop this ship holding her here from finding her mother. At the same time, both pushed their hands forward with such force that the ship began to lay over. All of a sudden, they both gave it all they had, and the pirate ship listed right on its side. Pirates hung onto everything they could, but they eventually flew off the ship right through the air and into the ocean. The ship became surrounded by a glowing green as Carly and Dizzy became stronger. Sails ripped apart, and stay wires that once held the tall mast in place snapped, one after another. The crew kept peeking over the rail. One last wire whipped through the air, and the mast snapped in two.

Noah yelled, "Stop! That's enough!"

They both kept going. The ship was now on its side. The grass that had grown on the vessel's bottom began to show. Moments later, the huge keel began to break the water, the sound of cracking wood filling the air. The ship's keel was the strongest part, but it snapped like a twig. There was no hope for the ship.

Noah and Cappy yelled, "Enough, enough!"

The bright green light from the two slowly dimmed as the once-fierce pirate ship made its way to the bottom. The British ship had lowered their lifeboats to pick up the pirates. They knew of the *Huntress*. Noah gave the command to lift anchors, and the crew began to haul them back off the ocean floor. They all looked at Carly and Dizzy. They had never seen Dizzy go that far, but now he had, and Carly had, as well. The crew was shocked but smiling. They knew Black had a problem now. The *Huntress* was well protected with their own wizards.

Noah pulled around to hail the captain on the British ship. He yelled, "Do you need help?"

The captain yelled back, "You have done enough. We will take things from here." He gave a wave, and Noah waved back.

The crew on the *Huntress* cheered, "*Huntress* rules the ocean!" But Dizzy looked tired and fell over. Carly dropped to her knee and fell to the deck. Cappy ran over and then kneeled down over both of them.

"Someone bring water!" he yelled. Whistler ran through the crowd, spilling most of the water before he made his way over to Carly and Dizzy and handing Cappy what was left. Cappy just looked at the man as he caught his breath. They had let themselves out of control. But thankfully, no one was hurt, and the queen's ship was safe. Noah yelled down to Hunter to come and hold the wheel. Hunter came up and took the wheel so Noah could go see Carly and Dizzy. When Noah reached them, they were sitting up. They looked a bit beat up after sinking a ship.

He asked, "Are you both okay?"

Carly and Dizzy looked at one another and smiled. "Yes, we will be."

The crew helped them down below to have the ship's doctor take a look. Noah yelled up to Hunter and Simon, now both up on the helm deck, to drop the sails and drift for a while.

Hunter yelled to the crew, "Drop the sails and tie them off! We will drift for a while."

Cappy pulled Noah to the side to have a talk. Cappy looked worried. Cappy looked at Noah with fear in his eyes.

"What is wrong?" said Noah. "You look very worried."

Cappy finally spoke. "We need to drop anchor and let Carly

and Dizzy rest. We don't know how much this hurts them to use such powers and then just fall." He waited for Noah to say something—anything—at this point.

"You're right," said Noah, "but Carly will not be happy with this, and we need to talk with her and Dizzy about going too far sinking that ship."

Cappy nodded and said, "That's a talk we must have, but not now."

Noah walked out on the deck and said, "Crew, I have something to say."

They all turned, stopping what they were doing. Hunter and Simon wondered what had changed. Noah spoke, and the crew stood silently, listening.

Noah said, "We will be staying another night. Carly and Dizzy seem to be very tired or sick. We are just not sure yet."

The crew looked worried. Noah could see this. He smiled and said, "They will be fine. I have seen Carly look this way before."

Noah turned, and his smile was gone now that the crew couldn't see him. He had seen Carly get weak after using her powers, but not like this.

Noah turned to Hunter and Simon and said, "Drop the anchor, and have the crew check the entire boat out. Make sure it's ready for another battle, if needed." Then Noah went to his room to read more of the ship's log.

Cappy sat with Carly and Dizzy.

Carly opened her eyes, looked at Cappy, and asked, "Did we jump through time already?"

"No," said Cappy. "We needed to make sure you and Dizzy were okay before doing that."

Carly went to sit up, saying, "I'm fine." But before she could sit all the way up, she fell back to her pillow.

Cappy told Carly, "You rest. We will jump when you and Dizzy are back to your normal selves again."

Dizzy was still sleeping. No one on the ship really knew much about who he was or where he came from. But one thing was for sure—he needed some rest right now. Cappy headed for the deck and began working on spare sails, never know when you might need one the way things were going. Hunter and Simon helped the crew do more repairs they had put off so they could go after Black and his gang. Everyone on the ship was just doing his or her own thing, making the *Huntress* perfect in every way. Some touched up the paint by hanging off the side of the ship. The ship was fairly new—other than all the wood that had been replaced. All the comforts of a hundred years into the past. The next day, the crew was woken by breakfast once again.

Cappy slept in a chair down below where Carly and Dizzy rested. He was very worried about the young kids. He had not seen Carly so drained of all her energy before. Simon was working on the charts when it came to him. They were in the past but still off the Forbidden Islands. The island just looked so different back then. Simon ran by Bell's crew and into Noah's cabin. Hunter saw him and followed. Simon barged through the door, Hunter not far behind.

"Noah!" Simon yelled.

"Simon, calm down," said Noah. "What is wrong now?"

"Nothing," said Simon.

"Then why are you looking like a crazy person?" Noah laughed.

"Noah—" Simon couldn't get the words out fast enough. "It seems that when we jumped though time, we only went back in time."

"What do you mean?" asked Noah. "I don't understand what you are trying to point out. I know we went back in time." Noah looked at Hunter, shaking his head.

"No, Noah," Simon said, getting frustrated. "You don't understand. We are home but hundreds of years or so earlier in time. The islands we've been looking at are the Forbidden Islands."

Noah stood up. "You mean we are right where we started?"

"Yes," said Simon.

"But Carly said we could jump anywhere." Noah looked a little confused now.

"We can, but we just haven't for some reason. I don't know why," said Simon.

"Now, why would Black keep coming back here?" asked Noah.

"Who knows?" Simon said. "But we need to find out how to move forward in time—sooner or later—to get home."

"Well, Simon, we're not going anywhere until we get Bell and the *Drifter* back."

Hunter looked at Simon and said, "He's right. We need to get the crew back their captain."

Simon looked down and softly replied, "I know this. But Carly needs to work on how to get home, as well."

"Have you been to see Carly this morning?" asked Noah.

Both Simon and Hunter shook their heads. "No, we haven't."

"Well, this will have to wait. I have to go down and see how she and Dizzy are. Simon, keep working on this, and Hunter, get the crew to ready the ship. We will go in the direction Black was last seen."

While up on the deck, they could see the British ship repairing their mast. They laid anchor in the distance. They must have worked through the night. It was no easy task standing a mast back up out at sea. Noah could see the crew standing on the boom of their forward mast. They were untying the rope used to lift the aft mast back into place. Noah knew they would be there a while, fixing all the damage from the battle. On the *Huntress,* the crew swabbed the deck, cleaned the *Huntress* up, and made her look fit once again. They took much pride in the ship. Noah headed down below to check on Carly and Dizzy. The ship had a strong smell of dampness this morning. They must have taken on some water in the fight. As Noah rounded the corner, he saw Cappy sleeping in the chair by Carly's side.

"Cappy," Noah called. Slowly, Cappy opened his eyes. Carly and Dizzy opened theirs, as well.

Carly asked, "Did we jump?"

Noah looking at her and Dizzy just listening.

"No, Carly, we cannot do that without you."

Carly smiled and said, "Well, then, let's get going!"

"Slow down, young lady," said Cappy. "How are you feeling this morning? And how are you, Dizzy?"

They both sat up with a smile. "Great!" Carly and Dizzy both spoke at the same time. "Something smells good!"

Noah and Cappy laughed. "Well, at least they're hungry," said Cappy.

They all went up for some food. The whole crew feasting was a nice thing to see, thought Noah. The day was sunny and warm.

"Great morning," said Cappy.

The queen's ship still laid anchor in the distance. Noah began to wonder how long her ship would be staying. Maybe they were having a hard time repairing the ship. Noah would keep his eyes on them and maybe send a few of his men over to lend a hand if needed.

A little later, the crew had finished all that needed to be done—*Huntress* was perfect once again. They finally had time to relax and maybe have a little fun, as well. While the crew kicked back, enjoying the great weather and a cool breeze, Whistler went down below. It wasn't long, and Whistler had a surprise for the crew—he ran back with a viola. Noah looked down as Whistler slid across the deck, trying to stop. His feet came right out from under him, and he landed on the deck. The whole crew laughed. Cappy could barely breathe after seeing that! Whistler stood up, smiling as he pulled the viola out and began to play. The whole crew stood clapping as Whistler played them a tune. It didn't take long, and they were swinging arm and arm around the deck. Cappy walked over to Carly and reached for her hand. Smiling ear to ear, she reached out. Noah and Simon watched Cappy and Carly dance away. Noah and Simon were happy for Carly. The ship's cook had heard the tune playing, so he made some snacks and brought them up on deck. Everyone ran to grab a piece of the cook's surprise before they were gone. Things were great. Not one of the crew thought about anything but fun. Hunter was dancing, as well. Now, that was something to see. Noah turned to look in the distance, wondering where Black and Ile had gone. *Maybe the Huntress will get a break for a while*, he thought.

The Wizard Keeps His Promise

Noah went below for a while. He needed to be alone. The young man really had his hands full but seemed to be holding up. He sat down on his bed and lay back. Noah thought of the talk he'd had with his mother—so many unanswered questions. He reached inside of his shirt and pulled the gold medallion out. He hadn't taken it off since he and his mom had opened the chest. Noah sat up and leaned forward for a moment. He missed home. After gathering his thoughts, Noah made his way back to the ship's helm, thinking that he had better check on the party he was missing out on. He seemed to walk right by the party, not paying any mind. He turned and climbed the ladder to the ship's helm. After the short climb back up to the helm, Noah turned to see that the British ship still in the distance. After taking a quick peek with the spyglass, he decided that it looked like they were getting ready to leave. Before Noah could turn back around, Simon and two others from the crew dumped buckets of water over his head and ran. Noah laughed as water poured down the back of his shirt. The young captain felt much cooler after that. Whistler was playing music for the whole crew, just having a blast. The cook had gone back to the galley, needing more snacks. The crew had eaten all the food. Not a care in the world, for the moment at least. That's when it happened.

The sky became dark and the air grew cold. Carly looked at Noah and the rest of the gang. They knew what was coming. The sky become so bright the crew could barely see. Then, a gust of fierce wind surrounded them, followed by a flash of light. There it was—*Dark Spirit*.

Simon said, "They didn't waste any time."

Black didn't hold back from firing on the British ship. Smoke filled the air within moments as they looked off into the distance. Black had caught the British ship and its crew off guard. Once again, the queen's ship was in trouble, and the *Huntress* would be right in the middle of yet another mess. Hunter and some of the crew ran for the cannons, down the stairs and through the ship. They just couldn't get there fast enough.

Hunter yelled at the crew to push the cannons out and prepare to fire. Noah tried to look in the spyglass to see what was happening. He could barely see them with all the smoke surrounding the ships. There was a bright red glow breaking through the cloud of smoke. *The wizard is ready to unleash,* Noah thought.

Carly and Dizzy still felt weak. "We must help them. They don't have a chance without us, Dizzy," Carly said, pulling Dizzy out of bed.

They both jumped out of bed and began to make their way up to the deck. Noah looked at the crew, he knew they were worried. They knew Bell was on Black's ship. There was silence among the crew.

Noah called out, "Haul the anchor, and raise the forward sail." Quickly, they did as he asked.

Hunter was down below, waiting for the order to fire cannons. He yelled up to Noah, "What side of the ship are we firing from?"

Noah yelled back right away, "Both!"

The crew looked worried. "Here we go again," said Simon. "Why can't we just strike one side?"

"I don't have time for this," Noah told Simon.

Huntress was really moving along now and getting closer.

Black still fired on the queen's ship as Noah went head-on right for the *Dark Spirit*. Smoke and cannonballs still filling the air, Noah got even closer. They soon would be able to touch if Noah didn't turn. Captain Black turned to see the *Huntress* heading his way. Carly and Dizzy were up on deck, ready to go for another round with the wizard.

Simon yelled, "We're going to hit them!" Simon grabbed onto the nearest thing and held on for dear life.

Noah spun the wheel frantically as the *Huntress* went into a hard turn seconds before ramming Black's ship. *Huntress* was just getting ready to pass across the back of both ships. Noah yelled to the British captain to leave. Noah could see the sail going up on the queen's ship while passing them. They were pulling away. Black had stopped firing on the ship and ran to the back of his ship along with some of his crew. Black yelled to ready the stern cannons as he made his way to the helm.

Huntress just passing the stern of the *Dark Spirit*, Black and Noah staring each other down, both captains yelling fire at the same time! Cannons thundered one after the other. Within moments, the sound of wood breaking once again filled the air. Noah waved the British captain off as this all started. *Dark Spirit* took two hits right through the back of the boat, sending Black falling to the deck. Black stood up just as the *Huntress* was taking a hit herself. The wood was flying everywhere, then another hit on the *Huntress* right through the side of the bow and out the other.

Both ships taken heavy damage fast!

Black's crew made their way to the other side of the ship just as Noah cleared the *Dark Spirit*. Watching the queen's ship sail to safety, he began to turn the *Huntress* around, making his way back for yet another pass. The fight was just getting started. Both crews loaded their cannons as the ships got ready for a showdown.

Noah yelled, "Drop the sail!"

Noah was going alongside of Black and his ship. They would be face-to-face shortly. *Huntress* slowed to a stop as they slid down the side of Black's ship. They all just stared at one another. *Dark Spirit* and the *Huntress* lay silently now side by side, ready to battle. Noah and Cappy stared at Captain Black. Carly and Dizzy stared down Ile. Like the calm before a storm, the two ships drifted alongside of one another. Noah looked back at the *Drifter*, tied to a line behind Black's ship—a prize for Black. That made Noah burn up inside. Noah was ready to get this started. He'd had enough of this when a young man walked down the deck toward the wizard. He walked with his arms crossed and head down. Not a word was spoken. Both crews just watched this young man. When he reached the wizard, he turned and looked up, staring at Carly. The wizard laughed and Black, as well. Who was this young man?

Ile said loudly, "Carly, meet your twin brother, O."

Carly and Cappy's jaws dropped. Noah and Simon didn't know what to think.

"Yes, my child, we kept O so I could train him to be as powerful a wizard as I."

Just then, the young man gave Carly an evil look and quickly waved his hand, sending a bust of energy that threw Carly clear across the deck of the ship. Bell's crew looked very worried now, along with everyone on the *Huntress*. Cappy ran to Carly, followed by Simon and Dizzy. She shook it off and stood up. Carly walked back, looking very angry. The two ships were very close together—too close for comfort. Simon bit away at his fingernails. Black and Noah both knew only one ship would survive what was to come. Then Black's smile went away as he looked at his crew. Noah knew he was about to fire on the *Huntress*. Quickly, Noah yelled, "Fire, fire!"

The sound of thunder filled the air as the two ships began to battle. Being so close, neither ship missed. With every hole blasted into the two ships, flying wood filled the air. Both ships were relentless. The wizard's eyes began to glow. Carly and Dizzy went to their knees and angered beyond any point any one had ever seen before. She waved her hands and sent a large surge of energy flying at the wizard. The wizard, fast as he was, stopped it and held Carly off. O began to fight with Dizzy, and they were tearing apart the two ships as the four battled. Between the cannons and the wizards, both ships drifted apart slowly. Carly and Dizzy became weak. The wizard and O could see this, but so did Noah as he yelled to raise a sail. Cappy kept a close eye on Carly as he pulled the sail up and waited for the wind to move them out of harm's way. Cannonballs flew though the air as the crew ducked from debris and breaking wood. *Huntress* finally began to move away from the *Dark Spirit*, just to turn around and come by for another pass. Everything stopped for a few moments. The crew looked at one another as Noah started back toward Black's ship. This time, Noah sailed down the other side of the *Dark Spirit*, trying to weaken the ship. Cannons ready and moving fast, the *Huntress* once again came alongside the *Dark Spirit*. Noah and Black both gave the order to fire at the same time. *Dark Spirit* hit the boom on the *Huntress*, and it came down fast, heading for the deck—Whistler right under the falling boom. Whistler crouched and held his head. Carly swung around, and with one swipe of her hand, she pushed the falling boom to the side. It just missed Whistler. Whistler stood up and drew his sword with an angry look in his eyes. He turned and pointed the sword right at Black. Black looked as if he had just seen a ghost. Black yelled to stop firing, and the wizard turned and struck Black down for giving the order. After seeing that, Black's crew wouldn't dare stop. Both ships drifted apart once again, but not fast enough. Carly and Dizzy were beginning to lose. Ile and O fought harder to win the battle. Noah helped Hunter fire cannons now. Both ships were being ripped apart more and more every second. Carly was ready to pass out, and Dizzy was not far behind her. This would be over soon. They had not recovered from the last battle. Carly and Dizzy were barely hanging on. Ile and O were ready to finish them off.

Soon, the *Huntress* would be sent to the bottom. Just then, Sarah, with her hands in chains, came limping onto the deck and headed right for O and the wizard. They didn't notice her. She escaped to stop this fight but looked very weak, as well. Cappy tried to watch Sarah as the cannonballs flew by him. Cappy could see one thing different about Sarah—she had the angry look that Carly had when ready to burst out. Sarah lifted her hands with the heavy chains and let out a lightning surge of her powers, sending O flying across the deck and now trying to hold off the wizard. After such a burst of energy, she was failing, and the wizard was slowly taking all of them down. By now, the ships had taken a beating. Between the powers on both ships and the firing of cannons, the vessels were full of holes. Sarah was on her knees, barely holding herself up, when she began to shout out a handful of words from one of the scrolls.

The wizard yelled, "No, Sarah, stop now!"

But it was too late. She sent the *Huntress* flying through time before Ile could take them once again. The air became cold as strong wind circled faster and faster. *Huntress* began her jump to wherever Sarah sent them. The wizard fell to the deck. Sarah had stopped him. Carly watched her mother fade away as they disappeared, traveling through time. With one last glance, they were gone. *Huntress* spun wildly, and everyone hung on once again. Then, there was the splash. *Huntress* had landed somewhere. Slowly, the bright light and strong wind went away. They had escaped, but at what cost? The crew slowly stood up as the ship settled in the ocean. The sun was bright, and the water was calm. Cappy and Simon ran over to Carly and Dizzy. They were sitting on the deck.

Cappy sat beside them both. "Are you okay?" he asked. They both just sat there.

Dizzy slowly stood up. "Boy, was that something," he said.

Looking up at Dizzy, Carly asked, "What do you mean by that?"

"Well, I have never seen a wizard so powerful."

Carly stood up. "Yes, and now he claims this O to be my twin brother."

Cappy just stood there. He didn't know what to think. Noah was sitting up by the ship's wheel, wondering what this was between Whistler and Captain Black. He would have a talk with Whistler later. Moments later, they heard a foghorn. The whole crew stood up. The ship was sitting off yet another island. Simon ran over, with the spyglasses Noah was looking for this ship. Simon ran down to the chart room, grabbed the chart, and ran back. He was back on deck in seconds. Simon placed the chart down on deck for more room, looking very closely at this chart. He said, "We are home."

Noah turned toward Simon. "What do you mean?" he asked.

"Yes, Noah, we're sitting right off the Forbidden Islands from our time." The whole crew began to look around.

Hunter yelled out, "You're right! Look at the ship in the distance."

Hunter knew this ship and Noah as well, it was from their town. The *Huntress* lay dead in the water. One mast was lying on deck from the battle. The sails were torn everywhere. There were holes all down each side of the ship from the cannons busting the wood to shreds.

Cappy looked at Noah along with the rest of the crew. "What do you want to do?" he asked.

Noah looked out into the clear ocean before saying, "Let's go home."

Bell's crew came from the past. They were about to see many things they could never imagine.

Whistler yelled out, "Bring her home, Cap!"

Up went the last sail, and Bell's crew members, along with help from Hunter, were able to get *Huntress* limping toward home. Simon went to plot the course back in. Cappy and Hunter sat on the bow as the crew began to fix what they could while underway. They sailed very slowly now. Noah sent Whistler up in the crow's nest at the very top of the mast to watch for other ships. Noah was standing by the helm thinking what the town would say when they pulled in with a hundred-year-old ship.

Just then, Hunter yelled to Noah, "Wait until the shipyard sees this thing!"

They all laughed. "Boy, we have some explaining to do now," said Simon.

"Yes, we do," replied Cappy. "Yes, we do."

The Voyage Home

Noah yelled down to Simon. He needed a course for passing the shallow waters near the Forbidden Islands. This wasn't the *Drifter*. *Huntress* needed much deeper water to travel through, being such a large ship. Simon shortly yelled out what he thought should be Noah's new course to keep the ship safe. Time seemed to move slowly as they rounded the Forbidden Islands, hoping to stay in deeper water. There would be silence until the ship was safe. Shortly into passing through the shoal water, they felt a bump, followed by a harder bump right afterward. *Huntress* began slowing down. Noah quickly spun the wheel toward deeper water. They had passed too closely. The whole crew stayed silent, watching Noah fight the wheel. The ship began to pick up speed as it rolled slowly from one side to the other—but not before one last grind against the sandy bottom. Noah, with his heart in his throat, hoped they didn't run aground. Another twenty minutes of silence went by, waiting for the ship to hit once again. They were just coming out of the shoal water when they felt yet another bump. This time, they could feel the ship dragging across the bottom. Everyone ran to the rails. Looking down, they could see the ocean floor. Carly threw her hands up quickly, pushing for more wind. *Huntress* gave a creaking groan throughout the ship as she broke free. They had cleared the shoal water at last.

Once again, Noah shouted down to Simon for a course taking the ship right into the town's harbor. Simon took longer than he would, so Noah shouted down once again.

"Simon," he said, "now would be a good time."

Simon gave Noah the course. The crew felt the ship turn as they headed home. Cappy was up on the bow with Carly. She was still holding her mother's unopened letter. Cappy placed his hand on his young daughter's shoulder.

"Carly," he said, "open it when you're ready." She looked at Cappy with a smile and placed the letter back in her pocket.

They had hours before the crew could see the lights of the town. Noah would be pulling into town just at daybreak due to the speed they were holding. They weren't going very fast, but the crew didn't seem to mind.

Bell's crew couldn't wait to see the town. They were looking forward to taking a look into the future. Flat, calm water, just a beautiful ride after all they had been through. Hunter and Simon leaned on the rail of the ship, looking for the first sign of light coming from their small town. As time went on, they should have seen the lights from the small town in the distance. But for some reason, they saw nothing. The *Huntress* kept heading for home. Surprisingly, the ship was still floated even with all the holes in it. Time went on … and still nothing. Noah became concerned. The sun began to rise, and they could see the town in the distance. Smoke filled the air throughout the harbor. It seemed that something had happened. Noah looked at Cappy, and they both looked worried. Simon and

Hunter stood on the bow as they came up on the channel makers for entering the harbor.

Noah yelled down to the crew, "Drop all but one sail," the ship began slowing down.

They were now close enough to see the docks had been destroyed. Noah yelled down to lower the last sail as the *Huntress* began to drift into the dock. Quickly, the crew pulled all the dock lines out. They were heading right for the town pier—or what was left of it. Noah dropped the anchor to help stop the ship as it came closer. He could see the crowd of people coming down to catch the dock lines for the huge ship. The anchor splashed down into the water as the *Huntress* scraped along the broken pier. Whistler and rest of the crew threw the dock lines onto the pier.

Townspeople quickly put them onto cleats as Noah yelled to the crew, "Tie the lines!"

Watching closely, Cappy heard the thick rope stretching as the ship came to a stop. The lines were fastened, and the ship was safely at the dock.

Noah looked around at the shipyard, smoke still filling the air from what was left of the building that once stood on the dock of this proud, small town. There were houses in the distance that lay in pieces. Noah saw his father and Mary pushing through the crowd to reach the ship. Noah ran down to meet him. Carly was right behind, running for Mary. Noah finally reached his dad, and they hugged like they hadn't seen one another in years. Carly and Mary did the same. The crowd was in an uproar. Noah ran back on the ship and made his way to the helm, the highest place on the ship. Noah began to yell at the crowd, trying to silence them. They didn't hear him. Noah again yelled at the top of his lungs, and soon, they all stopped arguing.

Noah asked, "What happened?"

They all began to get loud once again.

Noah yelled, "Enough! Just one person would be fine to tell the story."

Just then, the mayor of the town came forward. He was a short, heavy man called Smith. Noah asked the crew to escort the mayor, Mary, and his father onto the ship for a chat. The crew pushed the crowd aside, all still wearing their swords. They brought the people on board to the chart room, where there was room for all to sit. Noah asked his guests to take a seat. One by one, they pulled up chairs around the table. Smith told Noah that, for some time now, they had been watching two small boats come into the harbor. At first, they didn't think anything of this. In time, the town found out that the men were selling gold there. After hearing this, Smith ordered the law to arrest the men for questioning. Well, the men would not talk. After the second day, a large ship—the *Dark Spirit*—sailed into town. The ship dropped anchor out in the harbor, and the captain, a man called Black, came ashore with some of his men. He asked for his crew that had been arrested. He wanted them back. I told Captain Black they were being held until the problem was resolved.

"Black looked at me with angry eyes," said the mayor.

Black turned and began to walk out with his men, but before reaching the door, he looked back and said, "You will be sorry for this." Then he left, laughing all the way out of the building.

Smith continued, "Shortly after, we ran out to watch them return to their ship. They began to haul anchor, so we thought Black was leaving. He wasn't. He made good on his promise. The ship came closer and turned to its side as the cannons began to fire, one after the other. The buildings on the docks were destroyed. The townspeople ran for the hills, not looking back."

Noah asked quickly, "Did anyone get hurt?"

"No," said the Mayor. "But Black, as you can see, sunk all the boats at the dock and destroyed any house close enough for his cannons to reach. For some reason, Black didn't sink the *Raven*."

Why? Noah wondered.

"Story has it the *Raven* survived a fight with *Dark Sprit*, as you all know," Mayor Smith reminded them. "It is a mystery to this day why Black let them go."

Noah then looked at his father. "Where's my mother?" he asked.

Noah's dad looked down at the ship's deck. "Noah," he said, "while you were gone, she became very sick." Noah's face turned pale instantly. "There was nothing the doctors could do, my son. She has passed."

Noah with tears in his eyes, Carly came over and gave Noah a hug she could understand after all the years without her mother in her life.

Mary looked at Cappy. "Well," she said, "is my sister alive?"

Cappy didn't say anything for a moment. Then, Mary asked again.

"Yes." Cappy said. "She has a son called O, as well."

Mary smiled, but Cappy did not.

"What is the matter?" asked Mary.

"She is in danger, and the wizard has control of her son called O. The wizard himself has trained the young man. I don't know how long he will keep Sarah," answered Cappy.

Having powers of her own, Mary insisted on going to help Sarah. Carly was happy to hear this.

Smith, looking into Noah's eyes, softly said, "You're our only hope."

Noah wondered how Black's ship left the Forbidden Islands and came to port. That was something he couldn't do, looks like the wizard found a way of changing that.

Mayor Smith said, "I will order the town to help repair the *Huntress*. The sooner someone stops this pirate and the *Dark Spirit*, the better."

Noah asked everyone to leave, including his father. He wanted to be alone. Noah told the mayor to have his crew of carpenters there early in the morning. Noah went to find Hunter. Hunter looked at what once was home. Noah leaned on the rail of the ship beside him.

"Hunter," he said, "post guards tonight and ready any cannons facing out into the harbor, just in case Black decides to come back." Hunter was very angry about what had been done to his home.

Noah turned and called Whistler over. "Have the men working on repairs, but just until sundown. They will need their rest."

Whistler gave him a nod and gathered the crew. They worked for some time, but sundown came quickly. The day had passed by quickly. Whistler yelled out to the crew of the *Huntress* to call it a day. So the men put away their tools and headed for the galley where the cook had dinner ready. Hunter was working below, fixing the cannons. Carly had to get him since he didn't hear Whistler tell the men the day was over.

Simon was in the chart room trying to figure out everywhere they had gone so he would be quick to help Noah with courses to hold while sailing.

After seeing Hunter and telling him the day was over, Carly headed down below with Mary and Cappy. Mary was happy to hear that her sister was okay—for the time being, at least.

Noah was in his cabin on the *Huntress* when he heard a knock.

"Come in," said Noah.

The door opened, and his father was standing there.

"Come in, please," Noah said. "Take a seat."

Noah's dad looked lost. He had lost his wife, and his town had been destroyed. Noah had been sitting in his cabin, thinking of his mother, as well. They were both speechless. Noah's father looked at him with a smile.

"Son," he asked, "how in the world did you get this ship?"

Noah told him the story. His dad could not believe his ears. Noah's father knew Noah well—the boy would not lie. He reached over and shook his hand. Then he stood up and said, "I will be here in the morning. The mayor has called the town down to ready your ship. Seems you have your hands full now."

Noah laughed. "That's an understatement," he replied. He went to bed after another long day.

Cappy and Carly told the whole story to Mary, and she headed home, as well. Mary was eager to be back in the morning with the townspeople. She didn't show it, but the thought of taking on that wizard sounded better by the moment. Cappy went to his room, and Carly did the same on the other side of the ship. Now, they would all sleep. Hunter headed back to the cannons, just in case.

Mayor Smith Keeps His Word

The next morning, the crew woke at sunrise. There was the sound of a crowd gathering on the pier. Slowly, the beaten-down crew members made their way up onto the deck of the *Huntress*. The whole town was setting up work benches and pulling out all their tools to fix the mighty ship.

Hunter ran down to wake Noah, who had not heard the crowd. Hunter banged on Noah's cabin door when it just opened on its own. Hunter gave one hell of a knock to break the door open.

Noah jumped up quickly. "What is wrong?" He asked.

Hunter laughed. "Nothing, my friend. Come look outside."

Noah dressed quickly and ran up on deck. He could not believe his eyes. The mayor had kept his word, and the whole town had shown up. Trucks were backing onto the dock, dropping logs for new planks. They crashed to the ground, rolling against one another. From there, the men and women stripped all the bark off, making the logs smooth for cutting. Then, another group began to shave the logs flat for the planks that would be needed to fix the huge holes in the bow of the *Huntress*. The crew started working on the mast and boom, as well. The boom that held the sail on the back mast was split from battle. So they lowered it down to the deck and then pulled out a spare boom they had lashed to the rail of the ship. This boom had not been damaged. With long ropes and pulleys, they pulled the new boom up back onto the mast. Then fastened it well for the sail to hang from, hoping for no problems later on. Noah was very happy to see all of this work moving so quickly. Cappy told the men and women how long to make the planks he needed. They began to make just what Cappy asked for. Hunter stood on one of many rafts surrounding the ship. There were many carpenters on the rafts with Hunter. Cappy and the crew passed down the new planks as they needed them. Hunter and the carpenters held the planks in place as others screwed them to the ribs of the ship. One by one, the planks began to fill the holes in the bow of the *Huntress*.

It had been a long day, and night was setting in. Noah thanked all that had helped for the day. They all shouted out, "See you in the morning, Cap!" Then slowly, the crowd disappeared.

No one had seen Carly or Dizzy that day. Come to find out, they had spent the entire day studying the book and scrolls.

No one had seen Simon, either. He'd spent the day charting new courses. But when Noah walked in on Simon sleeping at the chart table, he saw something interesting. It seemed that Simon had found an island on one of Bell's charts. The island was marked with a skull. That had been the island Noah had read about in the ship's log—where the pirates went when they were not sailing the ocean. This was a place where nothing other than a pirate ship was allowed. From what Noah had read in the log, other vessels were sunk on the spot. Noah kept this in mind for the future. This was a place he might have to visit. Noah went back to his cabin to read more of the ship's log. Noah had hoped Bell had written something more about this island.

Carly and Dizzy slept right where they'd spent the day studying, and Cappy sat out on deck, looking at the town that was now in pieces. He shook his head and went to bed. Tomorrow would come soon.

Hunter was down with the cannons once again. It seemed to be his new bedroom. Yet another day had ended.

Morning came as Noah woke to the sounds of hammers and saws. He sat up slowly, tired from so much in such a short time. Noah dressed up and made his way to the helm, the highest place on the ship. There, he could see all the work being done. The crew had just finished the mast repairs and new sails where needed as well. Most of the carpenters were off the rafts. There were a few, including Cappy, making the finishing touches.

Hunter ran up to Noah, looking surprised. "What is it, Hunter?"

"Do you see the six men standing by the rail of the ship?" Hunter asked.

Noah turned. "Yes, what about it?"

"Noah, that's their ship!" Hunter pointed.

"What do you mean?" asked Noah.

The men stared at the *Raven*, not taking their eyes off the ship.

Hunter looked at Noah. "They were on that ship when it was attacked by the wizard."

Noah speechless looking at Whistler standing with them! What was between Black and Whistler? Had they met before?

Noah looked a little lost for the moment. "Then that would mean they are from here," said Noah.

Hunter looked at Noah. "Yes, but over a hundred years ago. The tall one was the mate on the *Raven*, according to Bell's crew. I guess the captain told them to leave the ship, thinking they would not survive. But the small boat jumped through time with the *Dark Spirit*. That's how Bell found them floating around and made them part of his crew."

Noah said, "What if we asked the mayor to put the *Raven* back doing what she was made for?"

Hunter asked, "What are you saying?"

Noah turned to Hunter and said, "Chasing pirates."

Hunter smiled. "Now that's a good idea."

Noah told Hunter, "Have the mayor and Mary, along with

the rest of the *Drifter's* crew, come to the chart room at noon. We will ask for the *Raven*. Don't forget to bring the *Raven's* crew, as well."

Hunter replied, "Will do, Cap. And by the way, the mate's name is Mason."

Noah smiled and said, "Hunter, you mean Captain Mason. He just doesn't know it yet." Hunter laughed and went to do as Noah asked.

The day went well. The crew and townspeople had fixed the *Huntress*. The trucks came down, carrying supplies for the *Huntress*. They slowly backed the trucks up to the ship. Then, men lined up to hand supplies over the rail of the ship for the voyage. The crew stored them as each box came aboard. Noon neared, and the whole gang that Noah had asked to meet arrived one by one. They all pulled out chairs at the chart table once again—all sitting there waiting to see what it was Noah wanted to speak of. Noah walked into the chart room, looking at the mayor. Noah, reaching out for Mayor Smith's hand, finally spoke.

"I would like to thank you on the behalf of myself and crew for all the help," Noah told them all.

Smith stood up, looking at the young man. "We need you, Noah. You're our only hope that this don't happen again. We will fix the ship again if needed."

Noah's smile went away. "Mr. Mayor, I want you to pull the *Raven* up to the dock."

"For what?" Smith asked.

Noah was very blunt. "That man sitting across from you was the mate on that ship, and the five others to the side of him were on there, as well. You see, Mayor, they were told to leave the ship. The captain was trying to save as many as he could, as you know."

Smith looked at Noah, confused as to what he was saying. He knew the stories. They were from over a hundred years ago.

"They had thought the ship would be lost. Mason and a handful of others went down in the dory. But when Black jumped though time, they went with him by being too close. Then, Captain Bell of this ship found them floating around in the middle of nowhere. So they became part of Bell's crew."

Smith, with his eyes wide and jaw dropped, mumbled, "The stories are true …"

Mason was stunned by this. He did not know Noah knew of this.

Smith, looking like he had seen a ghost, finally said, "They are the missing we speak of?"

"Yes," replied Noah, "they are."

Smith paused for a moment and gave Noah his answer. "I will have the ship brought to the dock and prepare it for Captain Mason, but this will take more time. We will send trucks to the old coal mine in the hills to retrieve all the barrels of gunpowder for the *Raven*. The ship would need a lot before getting under way."

"That's fine," said Noah. "We are leaving with the hope that Captain Mason and his crew are not too far behind."

Mary asked to sail with Noah. He'd known that she would ask.

Noah turned to Mary. "The *Raven* will need a wizard also. It would not be a good idea to have all the wizards on one ship."

Smith looked at Mary like she had three heads.

Noah laughed. "Mr. Smith, do you have a problem with this?"

"No, not at all," Mayor Smith spoke quickly.

Noah asked Smith to look for volunteers for the crew on the *Raven*. Smith said that he would get the word out right away. He didn't see it being a problem.

"Good luck, Noah!" Smith yelled out as he left.

Mary said good-bye to Cappy and Carly, all hugging at once now.

Noah told Carly, "Make sure Mary copies all of the scrolls you took from the wizard."

They all left, and Noah was alone. He rested for a while. Soon, he heard the *Raven* bounce off the dock as the townspeople tried to tie the big ship down. Mason yelled at them not to damage his ship. Noah started laughing. *Well, that didn't take long,* he thought. Mason took that command on very easily. Noah went to lay down. The crew had finished putting everything away, and the *Huntress* was ready to sail once again.

Before nightfall, Noah rounded up the crew on deck. There, he told them when they would leave. As Noah went up to the helm, the crew stood silently, waiting to hear when it was they were going to start the voyage. The crew was ready to leave right then and there. They all wanted another shot at capturing the *Dark Spirit.*

"We leave at midnight!" Noah yelled at the top of his lungs. They all cheered. Carly had that look in her eyes … the look of payback on that wizard again.

Simon and Hunter smiled. "Well, Simon, here we go again," laughed Hunter.

There was no talking after that. The whole crew—other than the guards—went to bed. They had only a few hours to sleep.

Heading Back into the Past

With the crew sleeping for their short nap before leaving at midnight, Mason over on the *Raven* still had the crew working through the night. Mason didn't want to be too far behind Noah just in case they needed him.

It wouldn't be long, and it was almost midnight. It seemed like the shortest sleep ever. Noah woke, and the cook had coffee ready for the crew. They had a great cook—the old man really looked out for the men on the ship. Noah went to wake Cappy, but as he walked in his room, Cappy rolled over and just looked at the tired young man.

"I'm up, my boy," Cappy groaned.

Noah went on to wake Simon, who was sleeping with charts under his head—still in a chair from earlier. Noah gave him a shake. It took a few shakes, and Simon was up.

Noah told Simon, "Wake the whole crew, and get them up on deck."

The ship was silent, but not for long. You could hear the crew running through the *Huntress* to reach the deck. Noah got up by the helm to wait for all the crew to arrive. But just then, Noah heard his name called out from the dock. As he turned his head, there was his father. Noah ran down and jumped onto the dock.

"Father!" Noah called out. "What are you doing here? It's late."

His father told him he wanted to say good-bye. Noah looked sad. "I am very proud of you," the father told his son.

Noah smiled and said, "I must go. The crew waits." Noah's father walked away.

Mason—now Captain Mason—jumped down to see Noah. Mason walked over while Noah watched his dad fade into the distance.

"Noah!" called out Mason with a smile. "I wanted to thank you once again."

Noah looked at Mason and said, "No, thank you."

Carly jumped down to say good-bye to Mason, as well. She handed him a hat.

"What's this?" Mason asked, looking at this hat she gave him.

"Well, Mason, the way I see it, every captain should have one. Good luck, Mason, and take care of Mary for me." Carly looked sad. Mason told her not to worry—he would do just that.

Carly handed Mason a bag with copies of scrolls for Mary.

"Make sure she gets this, Mason, or you won't be able to jump though time," she said.

"Thank you, Carly." Mason smiled once again.

So there stood Noah and Mason on the dock, shaking hands and wishing each other good luck. Then they turned and walked away.

Noah was back on the *Huntress*, heading straight up to the helm. The crew waited for orders.

Noah yelled out for them to take the lines off the dock, setting the ship free. With no engine, Noah needed help turning the boat.

"Carly and Dizzy!" yelled Noah. "Would you two give a hand and spin the ship? And by the way, maybe some wind in the sail to get us moving would be nice."

They both smiled. Carly's eyes began glowing green then Dizzy's as well, the ship began turning slowly. Just as the ship faced in the direction Noah wanted, the sails rose and began to fill with wind conjured Carly and Dizzy. The ship began to move slowly. Now with enough wind, Carly and Dizzy let nature take over.

Huntress headed out of the harbor, passing the channel markers. They all could see the crew of the *Raven* waving them a farewell. As the ship left the harbor, Cappy and Carly headed for the bow. That was the best place to sit and watch the stars. They all had hours before reaching the Forbidden Islands. Now, with the crew putting all the dock lines away and tying everything down in case of bad weather, there was time to take a breath and enjoy the ride. Simon yelled out a course for Noah, and it was smooth sailing from there for a while. Everyone was just doing their thing, playing cards or whatever they did when there was nothing to do. But just then, Simon yelled up yet another course. The crew didn't realize that hours had passed. Noah turned the wheel, and once again, they were heading for the shoal water. That only meant one thing. Shortly, they would jump or run into Captain Black. The sun rose, and through the shallows they went. It was a beautiful day with great wind for sailing; you could see for miles. Captain Black was nowhere in sight. Noah called for Carly. She was back on deck in a moment with her scroll in hand. She held her mother's letter—still unopened. Noah gave Carly a chance to put the letter in her pocket, and then she gave him the look.

"Okay, Noah," said Carly. "Here we go."

Carly's eyes began to glow as she spoke out the words of the scroll. Nothing happened. She looked angry.

Dizzy walked over and smiled. "You forgot that last word, Carly."

Carly's eyes glowed, and she spoke the words once again. The wind became cold and spun around the ship. Then, the bright light became stronger until they could not see. Just like that, they were gone!

To be continued ...

About the Author

John Verissimo has been a New England fisherman by trade for over twenty-five years. He was born on November 4, 1967, in New Bedford, Massachusetts, a seaside city known for its whaling industry heritage and made famous in Herman Melville's novel *Moby Dick*. He was drawn to the ocean at the age of fifteen. After twenty-six years of fishing waters from off the coast of Martha's Vineyard and Nantucket to the Hague Line of Canada, he decided to make a change to the ferry industry. As fate would have it, he found himself in the middle of nothing less than the historic event we all know as "Miracle on the Hudson." He continues to reside in New England.